Phyllis Walters

ANGEL'S JOURNEY
A Life Behind Bars

Angel's Journey

DEDICATION

I would like to dedicate this book to Angel Morgan who has passed through many stages in her life behind bars.

Let us not take our freedom for granted but be grateful for the women who have found God's purpose for their lives, despite their circumstances.

ACKNOWLEDGEMENTS

It was the hand of God that inspired me to write this novel. He urged me to continue when life's roadblocks seemed to pose an insurmountable impasse. I thank him for not giving up on me when I resisted his directive and felt stuck in the belly of the whale.

I am immensely blessed to have the constant encouragement of my patient husband, Dan Walters, who believes I can achieve anything I make up my mind to do, and more. I apologize for all the time away from him required to complete this heartfelt story.

I would be remiss if I didn't thank the Writers League of The Villages (WLOV) for providing me opportunities to learn, to introduce my books to our membership, to our community, and to social media sites.

I am grateful to the members of the Creative Writers Critique Group, led by Mike Doyle, for their honest, valuable feedback as I developed and revised chapter after chapter.

Lastly, I thank my illustrator, Bob Hurley, whose cover designs compel the readers to purchase my novel, and for my editor, Dr. Diann Schindler, whose expertise and drive for perfection brought out the best in me.

CAST OF CHARACTERS

In order of appearance

Dr. Rosie Klein	Forensic Psychologist
Daisy Marigold	Prison, Case Manager
Angel Morgan	Prison Inmate
Ruth Wayne	Dr. Klein's Office Manager
Bucky Walker	Dr. Klein's Husband
Ron Thompson	F.B.I. Agent
Caroline Wexler	Prison Chaplain
Dr. Josephine (Jo) Andre	Prison Medic
Verna Mitchell	Corrections Officer
Wes Hall	News Paper Journalist
Stella Gump	Daisy's Roommate
Travis Gump	Attorney
Devon Gump	Attorney
Thadd Holland	Lucas County, Sheriff
Liza Cunningham	F.B.I. Agent
Bonnie and Clyde Tipton	Paroled Sex Traffickers

Additional Characters

Angel's Siblings	Amanda, Greg, Mike
Dr. Rosie's Sons and Wives	Christopher and Lynn; Stephen and Louise
Dr. Rosie's Grandchildren	Josh and wife Janie; Beth, Oliver, Dottie

Editing/Design by: Diann Schindler, Ph.D.
at Diann Schindler Editing Services
DiannSchindlerEditor.com

Cover Design by: Robert Hurley
at ImpressionsBookDesignServices.com

PRINTED IN THE UNITED STATES OF AMERICA
ISBN: 978-0-9991375-5-0

ANGEL'S
JOURNEY
A Life Behind Bars

by

Phyllis Walters, Ph.D.

Inspired by a True Story

TABLE OF CONTENTS

Angel's Journey

CHAPTER ONE

The Case Manager

"Good morning, Mrs. Marigold. This is Dr. Rosie Klein. I've been communicating with Angel Morgan. Many years ago, I was appointed to evaluate Angel's competency to stand trial when she was charged with murder in Lucas County, Ohio. That is how we met. About four years ago, she was on my mind. I reached out to her, and we became pen pals. I understand that you are her case manager. Do you have a few minutes to talk?"

"Yes Dr. Klein. She told me about your relationship. and I've been expecting your call." I am her third case manager. I've been employed here at Marysville for ten years. Angel has already served almost three times that. As you well know, she is serving life in prison for her role in those six Toledo murders. I must admit, I am not familiar with her specific background."

"Angel was just released from Juvenile Detention where she had spent four years for grand theft auto. She had been arrested while sleeping in a stolen vehicle. If she knew who stole it, she didn't tell.

"She was a runaway after years of neglect by her mother, abuse, and a forced abortion after being impregnated by her stepfather. She had nowhere to go, no friends, and no family to turn to. The world was a scary place."

"I had no idea of her suffering, Dr. Klein," Mrs. Marigold said.

"A couple of teenagers approached her as she sat on a bench outside a store. They struck up a conversation and appeared to like her. She decided to stay overnight with them and ended up a party to a week-long murder spree in Toledo."

"I can't thank you enough for sharing her traumatic past with me, Dr. Klein." Mrs. Marigold's voice wavered as she shook her head and blinked back tears.

"Please just call me Rosie. I'm actually calling about how to receive collect calls from Angel."

"It's easy, Rosie. The two of you agree on a time. Then on the phone, you will receive a recorded request from the Ohio Reformatory for Women in Marysville Ohio, asking if you will accept a collect call from Angel Morgan. I should caution you. The lifer inmates take turns using the phones, so their call time is limited to twenty minutes. If she calls and you can't take the call, it is likely others will want the use of the phone."

"Okay. Thank you. Aside from that information, how is Angel doing?"

"I would say she does quite well most days. There are days when her back and her joints cause mobility and pain issues. She is always responsible and proud of her work in the prison sewing workshop. She tries to appear cheerful when it is obvious that she is struggling to fulfill her shifts."

"Angel mentioned her physical limitations to me in her e-mails. Her back and joints are arthritic. She is a sensitive, caring person. She asks about how my husband is doing and never complains about herself or her circumstances."

"You are right about that, Rosie. She is a very caring person. Please call me Daisy. My mother loved flowers and then I married Mr. Marigold. Daisy Marigold laughed and continued. Angel is like a little mother to some of the young inmates. Because Angel is an assistant supervisor in the sewing workshop, she has contact with women who are serving brief sentences for prostitution or drug offenses. Angel also works closely with our Chaplain, Caroline Wexler, who refers inmates to her who are struggling with spiritual and emotional issues as well as those with addictions. Angel co-leads several support groups for them.

Some of those woman inmates have written her saying that she saved their lives. She scared them straight when they saw what poor decisions can result in for the rest of your life."

"Angel told me in a recent e-mail that she believes God has a purpose for her life. She explained to me that the inmates sewed two-million masks and twenty-thousand disposable gowns during the height of the pandemic. One last question, Daisy. I received the materials to be approved for face-to-face visits. Any suggestions for making the visitation special for Angel?"

"I would advise you to bring cash if you would like to buy drinks and snacks from the vending machines. The procedure is quite easy, and I can tell you that Angel will really appreciate it. Let me know when you are coming. I'd like to meet you."

"Thanks. I will do just that. I thought I might come on a Thursday afternoon rather than on a weekend when it is likely very busy. Meanwhile, if she ever becomes seriously ill or needs assistance in any way, please notify me."

"Send me your contact information. I would be glad to add you to her file as a contact person. I work closely with the inmates to assist them in adjusting to their prison sentences, and developing life skills that will help them if they are ever paroled or pardoned. But I am close to retirement. Angel will be assigned to another case manager next year. I will be sure to personally pass all this information on to my replacement. Is that okay?"

"Absolutely. Thank you for your time. I Look forward to meeting you soon." Rosie hung up and jotted down a note to let Mrs. Marigold know when she would be visiting.

***

Angel reported to her case manager's office. She wondered why this meeting was requested. She didn't think she had violated any rules lately. She tapped on the partially open door and announced herself. "Hi Mrs. Marigold. You wanted to see me?"

"Yes, Angel, I do." Mrs. Marigold beckoned to Angel to take a seat facing the desk where she sat. "Dr. Rosie Klein contacted me about how to receive collect calls from you. Is that something you would be interested in doing?"

"That would be great. We have been e-mailing back and forth for several years. Dr. Klein remembers me from when I was first charged with those murders. I told her I didn't remember her, but I don't remember much about that time in my life. Dr. Klein was appointed to determine my competency to stand trial, they called it. That's such a joke. My lawyer never intended to go to trial for me. He made a deal with the prosecutor. Did you know that?"

"No, I'm afraid I didn't know the particulars of your case. In the time you have been assigned to me, we have never talked about it, and I didn't see any reason to do so, unless you do now."

"Dr. Klein said she appreciates my honesty about not remembering her. She said I could have lied and told her how kind she had been to me. I don't lie. Don't need to anymore. When I was little, I lied to keep my family together when family social services would investigate us. It became a habit. There were lots of complaints about how my brothers and I were cared for."

"Well Angel, this goes to show that honesty can result in good things."

"Ha. It didn't help me back then, Mrs. Marigold. I testified against the shooters with the promise of a deal, and this is how I ended up. Life without parole." Tears streamed down Angel's cheeks, and she didn't bother to wipe them away. She sat with her arms crossed in front of her chest and rocked slowly back and forth.

CHAPTER TWO

The Office Manager

Rosie hung up and took a sip of her lukewarm coffee. She reached across her desk where her long-haired, Calico cat, Willow, sat perched. Rosie scratched softly between Willow's ears. She thought about Jocko, her black labradoodle and Luke who was a pit bull/lab mix. They died of age-related ailments. That left Rosie without a pet to comfort and protect her from disgruntled spouses of clients. The dogs also functioned as a distraction from her stressful role as a forensic psychologist.

Five years ago, Bucky retired from the University of Toledo, they sold their condo, and Rosie sold her practice in Summerhill, Ohio. As part of that agreement, she retained office space for life. For four years, she and Bucky lived six months of the year traveling in a luxurious glamper. That is a combination of an RV and a camper. They spent three months a year volunteering at an Apache Christian Boarding School in Arizona. From there they traveled three months visiting their kids who lived in California, Michigan, Ohio, and Florida.

The University begged Bucky to return as interim Athletic Director after his replacement came down with pancreatic cancer and died quite suddenly. They returned to Ohio and purchased their log home outside of Sylvania Ohio. Rosie resumed her forensic work and led two support groups at her old office in Summerhill. Dr. Seifer renewed her Friday lease of the office downtown. Ruth resumed managing her practice.

Her third and last dog, Champ, a Labrador and Husky mix, was not meant to be a substitution for Jocko and Luke. Champ's playful nature gave Rosie and her husband, Bucky, a reason to get outdoors and enjoy their scenic new property nestled in seven acres of dense woods.

At first it was difficult for Champ to adjust to the presence of a small, orange, and black, three-year-old cat who came with the property. The earlier owner explained that his cat would never be happy away from this environment, and so she stayed. Fortunately, Willow and Champ bonded nicely. Tragically, Champ died at the age of ten, from being poisoned, the vet said. How did someone get through the security gate at the edge of the long driveway and poison their dog? And, why? Now, having Willow close by helps relieve her anxiety caused by both a stalker and a recent Summerhill office break-in. Not that Willow could defend her the way her dogs would, but Rosie was sure Willow would warn her of impending danger.

Rosie's thoughts returned to Angel. She wondered why authorities never follow up with juvenile offenders who age out of detention centers. Angel had no one to guide her and no place to go when she was released. She did let it appear that she was staying at the Y.W.C.A. After those years in detention for being caught sleeping in a stolen car she wouldn't do that again. She was arrested for stealing it, although she denied it vehemently. She tried to explain to authorities that it was freezing cold out and she was homeless. They didn't believe her.

And so, being invited to be part of a small group of friends appealed to Angel. How could she know she was joining a gang of hoodlums, at least the men were. When they offered her a place to stay, she quickly decided her plan to hop on a Greyhound bus and head to a warmer climate for the winter could wait. Christmas was around the corner and the idea of being alone did not appeal to her. At least in detention, volunteers brought them warm, delicious holiday meals and small gifts.

Suddenly, Rosie's manager's robust laugh jarred her from her deep thoughts and piqued Rosie's curiosity. Ruth, who ruled Rosie's days before she sold the practice to her partners and scaled down to part-time, was the most competent, dedicated office manager she could ever employ. With Willow in her arms, Rosie sauntered down the hall to Ruth's desk. She glanced into the adjacent waiting area. There stood Rosie's one and only. Bucky Walker. Husband, companion, and best friend.

"What's going on up here, Ruth? I wasn't expecting any tall handsome gentleman." Willow jumped out of her arms and scampered toward Bucky.

"Ruth smiled and explained, "This beer salesman is waiting for you, Rosie."

Rosie glanced at Bucky and back at Ruth who was chuckling and giving Bucky a thumbs up gesture and a wink. Willow had wound herself around Bucky's feet.

The expression on Rosie's face reflected both her amusement and total confusion.

Bucky said, "I'll explain later, Precious. Not to worry. I haven't made a career change as a beer salesman. It's just an in-joke between me and Ruth." Bucky created Precious as his nickname for Rosie to let her know how he felt about her. He wasn't embarrassed to use it in front of Ruth who they had known for years.

Bucky and Ruth burst into laughter while Rosie stood there appearing perplexed.

Ruth swiveled around in her chair to face her boss. She plunged ahead with her story, "He called last week and disguised his voice. He demanded to be allowed to deliver a case of beer and wanted full payment. No joke. He told me that according to the invoice, Dr. Klein ordered the beer."

Bucky joined them and chimed in, "I had you going, didn't I Ruth?"

Ruth glanced at Rosie, who didn't appear the least bit amused, and said, "What's on your mind, boss? You look extremely preoccupied."

"I just hung up from Angel Morgan's case manager. I can't get my mind off the turn of events that led to her life sentence. First, the detention center released her without knowing how to contact her in the future. Then she believed that being with new friends would soften the blow of not having anyone who cared about her," Rosie said.

"Well, Precious, I know you want to see her and speak with her personally," Bucky said. "I would be glad to drive you to Marysville and just hang out in town while you spend time with her. Besides, you only came back to work part-time so it shouldn't be a problem fitting in the trip, right?"

"At Christmas time she likely has terrible memories and feelings of guilt. If I recall, all the murders occurred the week before Christmas, right?" Ruth asked.

"That is true, Ruth. Thanks, Bucky, I might take you up on your offer. She is supposed to call me, and I'll ask if she would like me to visit. It is too bad that Christmas gifts are not allowed, but someone mentioned to me that a photographer snaps a photo of the visitor with the inmate. Each receives a copy. Certainly, that is a gift Angel will appreciate, and I will too.

Now to get back to your story about the beer delivery man. What did you tell Bucky to do, Ruth?"

"I raised my voice to this aggressive guy who then became speechless." Ruth pointed her index finger at Bucky and continued with her explanation. " I said I can't imagine why Dr. Rosie would need that much beer, or any beer, since she doesn't drink it and we have no holiday receptions planned."

Bucky finished the story by telling Precious that he walked into her office with a box of local Esther Price Candy instead of beer, and Ruth nearly fell out of her chair laughing.

For the time being, Rosie's spirit was lifted. She leaned down, gave Ruth a big hug, and blew Bucky a kiss. She suddenly recalled seeing a two-pound box of Esther Price on Ruth's desk and wondered who might have given Ruth such a nice gift.

"Ruth, did you keep the entire box of candy to yourself? You know that my favorites are the dark chocolate, pecan turtles," Rosie said.

"Well, Precious, that was the day I brought home a box of turtles for you," Bucky blurted out before Ruth or Rosie could respond.

Ruth chimed in, "Tell me why he keeps calling you Precious, Rosie?"

Before Rosie could explain, Bucky replied, "When I met Rosie, being a young widower, I felt lonely and confused about my future. She immediately gave me a new, hopeful vision for my life. And so, I nicknamed her Precious."

Rosie reached out, took his hands in hers, and squeezed hard. She was grateful for his sweet spirit and his public devotion to her. She leaned down, picked up their cat, and placed her in Bucky's outstretched arms.

"Meeting adjourned. I see that FBI Agent Ron Thompson has arrived for our scheduled interview. He has some previously omitted information he said he needs to share regarding Angel Morgan," Rosie said.

CHAPTER THREE

The Agent

Agent Ron Thompson, of the FBI, stepped out of his dark, cobalt blue, unmarked Chevy sedan and approached Dr. Rosie Klein's office. He met Rosie many years ago when he was still an Ohio State Highway Patrolman. With Willow nestled in his arms, Bucky quickly bent down, grabbed his newspaper, moved out of the front lobby, and took a seat in the adjacent waiting room. Bucky remembered being introduced to Thompson and his wife at a charity golf event, and more recently playing softball against him. Rosie stood beside Ruth's desk and waved at Agent Thompson as he entered through the glass door.

"Good morning, Ron," Rosie said. "Nice to see you again. How does it feel to work for the feds instead of the State of Ohio?"

"It has its perks and then again, there's a downside to every job in law enforcement, Rosie," Agent Thompson said.

"I can imagine. Do you remember my husband, Bucky Walker," Rosie said? She stretched out her arm and beckoned Bucky to come and join them in the entry way. Bucky released Willow who jumped to the floor. The two men approached each other, nodded, smiled, and shook hands.

"Nice to see you again, Bucky. Do you still play softball?"

"Yes, but not competitively. Just community softball. We played against each other in a law enforcement tournament. It may have been in the Spring after we met."

"You're not in law enforcement are you, Bucky?"

"No. The University of Toledo law school brought me in to play shortstop, "Bucky said.

Rosie chimed in. "Bucky is modest, Ron. He is a Hall of Fame softball player. They thought he would be the law school team's ringer."

"I will take off and let you two start your meeting," Bucky said, abruptly moving the conversation away from his accolades.

"Okay. See you this evening at home," Rosie said. Bucky waved at Rosie, Ruth, and Ron as he left the building. He had parked across the street at the meat market in case he decided to shop.

"Let's go to my office, Ron. Can Ruth bring you anything to drink?"

"I just finished a big breakfast at Frisch's, so I think I will pass. Thanks."

Rosie, with Willow following close behind, approached her office door and opened it to allow Agent Thompson to enter before her and take a seat where he pleased.

Agent Thompson took his hat off and sat down in an oversized, scotch plaid, wingback chair. Rosie sat on the matching loveseat across from him. Since their relationship, over time, had become informal, she saw no reason to sit behind her desk. She did, however, place her legal pad on her lap to write notes regarding this new information.

"It has been quite a while since we first met, hasn't it, Ron? If I recall, you were the Ohio State Trooper who helped pull over and arrest Angel and the gang. I was appointed by Judge Kate Brown at the request of Angel's pro-bono attorney, Dan Singer, to evaluate her for Competency to Stand Trial. I read your arrest report and I do remember meeting for the first time at my downtown office in the LaSalle Tower.

"That's correct. Ron took his handkerchief from his right back pants pocket, bent his left elbow, sneezed into it, and dabbed his nose. "Sorry, Rosie. I'm allergic to cats."

"Oh, I am terribly sorry."

"Don't be. I will be fine." Ron proceeded to say, "I never could understand how Angel got tangled up with that group of hoodlums, Rosie. They cost six people their lives, and deep heartache to the families of the victims. Why was Dan Singer her attorney? He was a prominent Toledo defense attorney not a public defender. She had no money for his representation, right?"

"To answer your question, every few years, the Judges appoint an attorney in private practice to take a murder or rape case, pro-bono, rather than for defendants to use a public defender or represent themselves, pro-se. The attorneys aren't happy about that. It costs them billable hours from private clients."

"Okay. That makes sense. Doesn't seem like they would have much choice if they want to stay in the good graces of the Judges."

"Did you know that Angel and I are pen pals, well actually e-mail friends. You said on the phone that on the twenty-fifth anniversary of their six-day siege, you thought about me. Why is that?"

"That's right, Rosie. I thought of you. Wes Hall, the investigative reporter on the case, has a continuing interest in Angel's story. I had coffee with him last week. I told him I planned to call you. Have you seen Wes lately?"

"No. I just know he still works for the Toledo Blade and on occasion I see an article or story he has written in the morning paper. May I ask what made you think of us?"

"Yes. My memory of the events doesn't coincide with what I read in the transcript regarding the Prosecutor's closing argument at Angel's sentencing hearing. Wes published the Judge's findings, conclusions, and sentencing of all four defendants. I was left questioning how Angel could be sentenced to four counts of life without parole, when she was supposedly offered a deal for her testimony against the two shooters. Plus, I believe she never held a weapon."

"Angel told me she thought she signed an agreement for one murder charge when she met with her attorney and the prosecutor. They told her it would take the death penalty off the table, which is a bunch of bunk. No jury would have given her the death penalty once they heard of the physical and mental abuse along with neglect she suffered as a young child. As it turns out, one of the shooters received the death penalty and the other two gang members, James Abraham, and Song Lee, are serving the same sentence as Angel. The two of them were juveniles and the new Ohio law says they are entitled to parole hearings while Angel is not."

"Well, Rosie, when you met with her back then, did you think she could comprehend exactly what a life sentence without parole would mean? Did she know she had options?"

" We did discuss the charges she was facing and the sentences that could apply. Her deal was never discussed with me because it had not been offered during my evaluation. I saw her on six separate occasions. Her IQ was in the high seventies. It probably was deflated due to stress, lack of education, reading ability, and environmental deprivation. I wondered why her defense attorney had the Judge appoint me to evaluate her if he had no intention of going to trial. I don't believe a psychological evaluation is required when there's a plea agreement."

"Wow, Rosie, I find your examination to have been very thorough. Your findings would have been quite interesting to a jury. At least they were provided to the Judge for her sentencing, right?"

" Yes, and I testified. Were you in the courtroom for Angel's sentencing hearing following her plea agreement? The three other defendants were each sentenced after separate hearings before the same judge. Fortunately, the victims' families only had to testify once. That was painful enough and painful for spectators to hear."

"From my years in law enforcement, I can imagine. But, no, I wasn't there. I was in the courtroom for Angel's testimony against both shooters. It appeared obvious that she knew what questions she would be asked, and rehearsed what she was supposed to say. I wonder who coached her."

"I do recall seeing you in civilian clothes standing in the back of the courtroom. Were you off duty? I totally agree about Angel being prepped. She had a limited vocabulary and would never have used the words she expressed in her testimonies."

"Here's the thing, Rosie. She wasn't asked if she witnessed the shootings. It was assumed. She testified that she heard them bragging when they returned to the house and saw items they had stolen from the victims in four of the six murders. I don't think they took anything of value from their two friends when they ordered them out of the car at the quarry and executed them."

"I agree. Can you imagine that they killed their own friends?"

"Angel told me they thought the friends were going to narc to the cops. But Angel said that was just false. The shooters were becoming paranoid."

"Unbelievable, Rosie."

Rosie leaned forward and clasped her hands together in her lap. "What are you suggesting ?"

"I don't see how she could be sentenced to multiple counts of murder if she wasn't with them or didn't know their intent to kill. She could be convicted of obstruction, being an accessory, and other lesser charges, but not murder one."

"True. I plan to have her call me next week. Hopefully, I will get cleared to see her before Christmas. I don't want to question her online or on the phone. If the visitation room is bugged, so be it, I guess. I will inquire as to what she truly observed firsthand and what exactly she participated in. And I will ask who prepared her testimony."

"It probably won't make a difference, but Wes intends to write an updated story when next year's anniversary date comes around," Ron said. He stood to leave.

Rosie followed suit. She realized she had been so engrossed in their conversation that she had failed to take notes.

"Thanks for coming in Ron. I will get back to you after I see Angel. I would like to have coffee or lunch with you and Wes. Downtown works for me on Fridays."

"You still have your downtown office in the LaSalle Tower, I take it, Rosie."

"Yes, it is convenient to be by the Federal and County Courthouse on Adams Street, and near the Lucas County Jail. It is also nice for professionals who work downtown. I still see some of them or their family members as private clients either during their lunch hours or immediately after work. In the winter, the indoor parking lot with valet parking is a plus and not having to drive to the suburbs helps them, and me too."

"Gotcha,"

"By the way, you probably didn't know that Bucky and I have an RV. After he retired, before he became the interim athletic director, we bought an RV. We volunteered in Arizona at a Christian Apache boarding school. Then his replacement died of pancreatic cancer and Bucky has stepped in until they hire a permanent director."

Agent Thompson stood, and wiping his nose said, "You two are amazing. Thanks for your time, Rosie. If I don't see you, have a nice Christmas. I will take you up on lunch with Wes. Let's plan to meet between Christmas and New Years."

"Sounds good. And a merry Christmas to you and yours."

CHAPTER FOUR

Angel's Story

Angel left her case manager's office with a feeling of relief. Dr. Rosie did not abandon her. Angel has always felt as if she pushes people away or because of her past, they think she isn't a nice person. She stretched out on her bunk, grabbed her journal from beneath her pillow, leaned on her elbow, and began to write. *I am so grateful for Dr. Rosie's interest in me. She's more than a friend, almost like family. Well, the family I wish I had. I know I shouldn't look back and blame anyone but myself. I just wonder what I could have become if I had a mother and father who loved, guided, and protected me. Or at least if I had one loving parent. I was told by Chaplain Caroline that feeling sorry for myself contributed to me making such a mess of my life. I wouldn't have been on that bench outside the 7-11 store waiting for a Greyhound. I wouldn't have been so desperate that I'd go home with strangers for what appeared to be a chance for friendship. Or would I? Maybe I was just born a loser, useless, worthless, just like my mom and stepdad always said.*

Angel's thoughts were interrupted by the sound of the horn, signaling it was time for chow. That's what she called every meal, not discriminating between breakfast, lunch, and supper. She inserted her special pen into the journal to mark the spot where she ended and planned to write more at bedtime. She slipped back into her shoes and headed for the cafeteria.

Angel took her place at the end of the line and stood silently as the women moved forward to receive supper trays. Meals were never tasty, usually lukewarm whether they were supposed to be hot or cold. Angel's path was interrupted by Song, her co-defendant, who jumped in front of her as she always did. It wasn't so much that Song felt entitled. She just never got to where they were expected to be on time. That explains why Song hasn't worked in the sewing workshop where they all reported to work at 8:30 and sewed or packaged till 3:30. It took five days a week to meet their quota of completed products, be they Ohio flags, USA flags, or sports team flags. They worked steadily to avoid having to work on Saturday mornings. The powers that be, as the Warden and Supervisors were called, determined early on, that Song should be on the clean-up crew following all three meals, five days a week and one weekend a month. The daily hours totaled the same, but she worked later because of mopping floors after supper. Angel felt grateful that she had private time in the late afternoon to shower and read her Bible.

"How's it going?" Angel asked Song.

"As well as can be expected. My parents will be visiting me every weekend this month. They think it will lift my mood. They just don't get it. Nobody or nothing can do that when you face the same routine every day of your life. How about you? Any word from your mother or grandma?"

"Grandma is old and in poor health. She keeps me up to date with the family. Not my mom. She has no use for me. She is with her fifth husband. Well, her fifth live-in boyfriend. Like the Samaritan woman at the well."

"Who is that? Why is your mom at the well?"

Angel shook her head and kept her thoughts to herself. *Obviously, Song has no knowledge of the Bible. Should I go there? Tell her about Jesus? I should ask Chaplain Caroline for a Bible and give it to Song for Christmas. My mom sure could benefit from reading it. It must be horrible for both of them to face these gloomy days without starting each morning with God.*

They grabbed their trays consisting of watery tomato soup, grilled cheese, fruit cocktail, and a small carton of milk. The big, if you could call it that, meal of the day was lunch. Angel took a seat at a metal table with attached benches that provided room for five others.

Song sat across from her and asked again. "Tell me what you meant by your mother being like that woman at the well. I don't get it."

"There was a woman in the Bible who was scorned by all the other women. She didn't go to get the day's water supply until mid-day, long after the other women had gotten theirs. They judged her because she had lived with five men, some of whom were not her husband. She was not married to the man she now lived with. Jesus approached her and asked for water. She asked him why he was talking to her since the Jews didn't speak to the Samaritans. She pointed out that he had no cup from which to drink the water. He replied that he was speaking of living water. He told her all about her life and she couldn't believe that he knew those things. She realized he must be the Son of God and she ran off to tell the other Samaritans."

"Wow. That's quite a story. So, what you are telling me is that your mother has lived with five men. Did you know them?"

"Some of them I knew. Some came along after I ran away. You had such a nice family. How did you ever get involved with someone like James?"

"It is called love, Angel. Stupid, I know. Haven't you ever been in love?"

"I guess I can't say that I have. It took being in prison for me to know love."

"What on earth do you mean? Are you involved with a guard or something?"

"No. Of course, not. I mean Jesus. Chaplain Caroline introduced me to him. Now I spend my early mornings and late nights with him and never feel alone. There are times that I feel unworthy, but I never feel alone. He loves me unconditionally." Song looked at her quizzically.

The five-minute horn blared. Their conversation ceased as they quickly ate their food and returned their trays to the conveyer belt.

***

There was a tap on Angel's door, alerting her that she had a visitor. With a startled look, Angel who was stretched out on her bed, glanced up, saw Chaplain Caroline, and smiled. Angel said, "How about I come out and sit a spell with you Chappy. So nice to see you."

"I've meant to come sooner. I know it's been ten days or so. I got tied up with some new lifers and helped Mrs. Marigold with their orientation."

"I totally understand. You are always very busy."

"Angel, I'd like your help, if you are willing. Could you meet with the new women and me for an hour tomorrow?"

"Sure. I'm not in the sewing workshop this Saturday. Our government contract for the USA flags is completed and we don't get back to sewing Ohio flags until Monday."

"I've been meaning to tell you how proud I am of your work ethic, Angel, and your commitment to help other women adapt here."

"Thanks, Chappy. Do you remember when I first called you Chappy? I was being sarcastic. I hope you forgive me. It is my term of endearment for you now. Endearment! That's a word I just learned, by the way. I watched an old movie, Terms of Endearment."

Chaplain Caroline laughed and patted Angel's cheek. "I'm hoping after you meet the new women, you might agree to see them weekly, as a group, through the winter. Remember your first winter behind bars, so to speak?"

"Well, it was long ago. I think I remember that winter. On the other hand, I was so angry I couldn't see straight. I couldn't believe I got myself in this mess. Of course, at that time, I didn't blame myself. I had what you might call "victim posture." The "why me" syndrome. Without you, the medic, and the prison shrink, I'd never have made it." Angel said, her voice choking.

"Such a long road it has been." Chappy brushed the hair from Angel's eyes.

"I am blessed to have had you here for twenty-three or so years. I don't blame Dr. Bennett for moving into her own private psych practice instead of staying here once she had her PhD in counseling."

"Well Angel, I think I'll stick around another seven."

"That's good news. You were like twenty-five years old when we first met. Not much older than me. Now, you look a lot younger than me. Much prettier too!"

Angel's tone lightened. "I have some good news to share Chappy. Dr. Rosie Klein, the psychologist I've been e-mailing, is going to receive collect calls from me and come to visit soon. I told her when she first contacted me by snail mail that I didn't remember her. I didn't want to hurt her feelings, so I said I don't remember much about that time in my life, which is true. I was such a mess, and everything happened so fast."

"Having her as a friend is great, Angel. I'd like to meet her."

"She sent me two journals last Christmas and a women's devotional Bible. She asked me if I was gifting one of the journals to someone. I explained that I could really use both. One is my morning prayer journal and one I write in at night to talk out my feelings and thoughts about the day."

"Hopefully, your journals and your women's devotional Bible bring you peace and hope, Angel."

"They do, along with the support I receive through your Celebrate Recovery Program. I never would have believed it. What kind of hope can a woman have in prison for life? This past year I have learned to believe that God has a purpose for my life and it's not for me to understand. Trust and obey, right Chappy?" Tears of joy streamed down Angel's face.

CHAPTER FIVE

The Phone Call

"Good morning, Bucky." Rosie sat down at the kitchen island, greeted her husband with a kiss on the cheek, and handed him a cup of freshly brewed Boston Stoker coffee. "I am expecting a collect call from Angel. I gave our home phone number to her case manager, Daisy Marigold. I plan to put Angel on the speaker phone if you care to listen. There won't be any private conversation. I assume the outgoing calls from the prison are taped. Wouldn't you think?"

"Most likely. Why don't you ask the next time you talk to her case manager. Ron Thompson might know, too. Likely that prisons and law enforcement agencies all work the same way," Bucky said as he returned his wife's tender kiss and took a sip of the bold black coffee.

"I will do that. Why do you have your jacket on in the house?"

"I am going back to campus for an hour or so. The new Dean and I have some recruiting ideas to toss around with the coaches of the men's and women's baseball teams. Sorry to miss the call. Thought you would prefer the privacy."

"Okay. I will fill you in when you get back. Do you mind picking up a pizza from the Elbow Room? I love their crust. Just put the Anchovies on my side." Rosie laughed and Bucky frowned.

"No problem, dear," Bucky responded.

"I noticed you didn't call me Precious. I bet I know why. Could it be that anchovies are not on your favorite topping list?"

He threw her a kiss, patted her, and disengaged Willow from his ankles, then headed for the unattached garage. When they moved to their log house, they lost many of their creature comforts, such as proximity to the University, to Rosie's offices, and their attached garage. But, in both of their opinions, to have the acreage and a garage with a loft to serve as a home office was worth it. He recalled sadly how much their dogs loved romping in the Autumn leaves.

Just then the Reformatory call came through. "Yes, I will accept the call," Rosie said.

"Hi, this is Angel. Is this time okay, Dr. Rosie?

"Of course. So good to hear from you, Angel. How are you doing?"

"Well, pretty well. My spirits are up because I have gone back to praise dancing and teaching other women to do it. Did I ever tell you that I used to dance before my arthritis kicked in? Then my blood pressure went sky high and I got dizzy. Now I have medication and can dance again."

"I saw praise dancing at a weekend Beth Moore retreat, Angel. It was lovely. The dancers were barefooted, wore long, white, chiffon dresses and matching scarves. It was also sad. Seventeen dancers dedicated their performance to seventeen teenagers who were shot down at school by a mentally ill former student."

"I saw that on-line, myself, Dr. Rosie. We all cried and prayed for their families. It helped me choreograph our dances. But we don't have beautiful dresses, just tights and long-sleeved shirts. They won't let us have the scarves because they worry that we will hurt someone or commit suicide."

"Do they ever film you? I would love to see your performances. I doubt that you call them performances, right?"

"We call them praise dances since we dance to express our devotion to God and Jesus."

"Cool. Do you have a choir, Angel?"

"No. At our worship services, Chaplain Caroline shows videos of hymns with lyrics and beautiful scenes of nature. Some hymns are contemporary and make you want to raise your arms in the air. I am not the least self-conscious about doing that. I was in the beginning."

"That's great."

"I need goals, Dr. Rosie, and they won't let me take college classes on-line because I won't be getting out to have a career. Girls who have five years or less left on their sentences can do that. I got to settle for non-academic classes and hobbies. The praise dancing structures some of my evenings after work and Saturday mornings. I also love teaching, whether it is dance or Bible study."

"Are you leading a Bible study now?"

"No. We are through until after Christmas, which is too bad since it would give us things to think about rather than ourselves. Feeling sorry for yourself is useless, right?"

"Absolutely, Angel. Do you have any special friends?"

"Not really," Angel answered with a sigh. "My codefendant, Song, is not a Christian. I think she is into WICCA. She hides it and doesn't say much to me. She avoids Chaplain Caroline and even Doctor Jo. She meets with other witches secretly. The guards know it. They aren't fooled. They just turn their heads as long as they don't try to indoctrinate the rest of us or injure us in any way. Fortunately, she doesn't room with me. I have seven roommates. No privacy you can see."

"Another reason I wanted to talk to you is so we can set up a date for me to visit. Would you like me to do that? We can catch up on how you're doing and talk about whether there is anything I can do for you on the outside."

"Oh, my gosh! I would love you to come. I don't even know what you look like, and you won't recognize me, for sure."

"I heard that I could order lunch. Is that so?"

"Yes, but you must order it five days ahead and get approved for your visit about three weeks ahead. I would love a personal size pizza and tater tots. It is one of the options on the brochure."

"I will follow through, Angel."

"How is your husband? Has he had health issues?"

"He is fine. He takes medication now to prevent a heart attack and had a pacemaker inserted that monitors his heart beats. He offered to drive me up to visit you. He is very supportive."

"Tell him I said he has to stay healthy to take care of my best friend."

"I will do that, Angel. Have a nice weekend. It has been a pleasure talking to you at last."

"Bye, Dr. Rosie." Angel hung up and Rosie was hopeful that she could meet face to face with her before Christmas.

CHAPTER SIX

The First Visit

"Okay, Precious. The car is packed for our overnight stay at the Mt. Vernon Bed and Breakfast. There is no more snow in the forecast. It should be an easy trip. I will put Willow in her carrier in the back seat if you are ready to take off," Bucky said.

Rosie handed Bucky the cooler. "Since it is only twelve o'clock, we should get there in time to check in and leave our things and Willow in our room before we go to that quaint little Amish restaurant for dinner."

Bucky opened the car door for his precious wife. After buckling her seatbelt, Rosie said, "Don't you think it is great that the proprietor allows cats with their dander and all? I would hate to kennel Willow or leave her alone. I still can't get over losing Champ. Who would poison him?"

"We will catch the perpetrator, Rosie. The Sheriff said your jacket was found outside our gate. Remember when you left it on the back of your chair at the restaurant? It carried your scent and lured Champ to the poisoned meat just inside our property." Rosie wiped away a tear.

"I spoke to Angel's case manager, Mrs. Marigold, and she will be able to meet me tomorrow morning prior to my visit with Angel. If I provide her with Christmas gifts, she will find a way to get them to Angel. The prison rules don't allow for gifts to be given directly to inmates by visitors. I bought her a pair of Nike's that will be support for her feet when she works long hours in the sewing workshop. I also got her six pairs of short, white socks."

"Rules are sometimes made to be broken, when good intentions are at hand, Rosie. I admire your sweet, caring nature."

" Mrs. Marigold decided to review the case file. I know it will provide her with more insight into Angel's background. Oh, and I ordered pizzas and potato puffs for lunch just as Angel requested. My visitation begins at one o'clock tomorrow."

"I can't believe you are going to forgo your daily roasted chicken salad with feta and craisins. Just joking, Rosie."

"I can always count on you to lighten my path, Bucky. Thank you again for driving me there."

"My pleasure."

The Amish restaurant turned out to be just what the doctor ordered, so to speak. Bucky and Rosie were seated at a table for two in front of a crackling fireplace. The menu was limited on a weeknight, but their server, a blonde teen-ager, with braids and wearing a crisp white apron with red ruffles across the top, highly recommended the creamy, country casserole. She explained that it had both tomato and mushroom soup with noodles, ground beef, and shredded cheddar cheese on top. She wasn't wrong. Her tip demonstrated their approval.

*** '

The next morning Bucky drove Rosie to the prison. They were quite surprised that the entrance was not guarded. A sign directed them to the visitors' parking lot.

"I will wait until I hear it is okay for you to stay this early in the day. Call me before they have you turn in your cell phone."

"Thank you, Bucky. You're such a sweetheart. That is a good idea. I would hate to be standing out here in the cold until visiting hours."

Rosie got out of the car and walked up to the entrance with a large visitors sign above the door. The sidewalks and parking lot had been shoveled and salt was spread to prevent slipping. Rosie entered the building and introduced herself to the guard seated at a desk. His name tag read Officer Kensington.

"Good morning. I am Dr. Rosie Klein. I have an appointment with Mrs. Marigold and will be visiting Angel Morgan later."

Rosie produced her driver's license. Officer Kensington smiled, took the ID, handed her a visitor's badge, and a sign-in sheet. She signed her name, time of day, and who she was visiting. She noticed the titles of previous visitors were attorneys or pastors.

"If you want anything to drink, cold or hot, you need to purchase a vending machine card." Officer Kensington pointed to what looked like an ATM machine. "The first three dollars are for the card. Any money beyond that will go toward purchases. You don't receive change," Kensington said. He picked up his desk phone receiver and called Mrs. Marigold to advise her that she had a visitor.

Rosie followed Kensington's directions. She inserted ten dollars which left her seven dollars for drinks and snacks. She thought if Mrs. Marigold offered her brewed coffee now, she would not drink it at lunch. There would be plenty of money on the card to buy cold soft drinks and candy.

Daisy Marigold came into the lobby and greeted Rosie with a firm handshake. She wore a navy-blue blazer with an American flag on the lapel, a white turtleneck sweater, and grey flannel slacks. Her black boots had rubber soles and were ankle length. Her hair was auburn, shoulder length, with bangs. Rosie couldn't tell if she had a weapon in a holster behind her waistband.

"Good morning, Rosie. How was your trip and your stay at our local Bed and Breakfast?'

"Everything went very well. The country roads were clear, and the Bed and Breakfast was cozy. Our room had a gas fireplace. It took the nip out of the air. Tea bags, instant hot chocolate, K-cups, as well as a small coffee maker, and a microwave enabled us to sip hot drinks of our choice. The proprietors are very thoughtful. They directed us to a locally owned Amish restaurant for dinner."

"That's good to hear. Let's go to my office where you can get comfortable." Rosie laid her purse, shoebox with gym shoes and black socks, jacket, phone, and keys on the conveyer, then stepped through the metal detector door behind Daisy. She retrieved her items and suddenly remembered she was supposed to call Bucky.

"Excuse me, Daisy. I need to let my husband know he can leave now. Bucky is waiting to be sure I am admitted this early." She was surprised but glad they allowed her to keep her phone.

"That was very thoughtful of him, Rosie." Daisy stood aside as Rosie made the call.

"Thanks for calling, Rosie. I will head into town and check out the local breakfast hang-out. I think I can find the good old boys." Bucky laughed.

Daisy escorted Rosie to her office. "Make yourself comfortable. I made a pot of coffee. Would you like a cup?" Daisy was pouring coffee into her personal mug.

"Thank you. Just black, please."

Daisy handed Rosie a full mug with the prison initials on it and took a seat beside her. They placed their coffee on the small, wooden, glass top table between their chairs, crossed their legs and faced each other. Rosie noticed that Daisy's desk was against a wall and stacked high with three ring binders and file folders. Above the desk was a window looking out on an enclosed, wide, snow-covered courtyard. She recognized having just walked through it.

Rosie couldn't help but think, *"looking out from Daisy's desk probably gives her a reprieve from the drab walls and narrow corridors within this institution. I wonder if the picnic tables and chairs are for the corrections officers and staff, or whether the inmates have the privilege of sitting there. The walls surrounding it are high and it is doubtful that prisoners would attempt to escape."*

"I took it upon myself to review Angel's records, Rosie. They are separated by decades. The first ten years included her background and her activities in our facility. She had trouble adapting to our daily routine and making friends with other inmates. She was never disrespectful to the guards or employees, but she had anger issues triggered by any number of petty things, like if someone accidentally bumped into her. She acted very impulsively and ended up spending a lot of time in solitary confinement. She seemed to prefer that."

"Angel has been very honest with me about those years. Before her plea agreement, she doesn't remember spending a lot of time with me in the professional conference room at the Lucas County Jail. If she lied to me, I would have been less interested in getting to know her."

"I'm glad to hear that. So many inmates create false backgrounds to attempt to impress authority figures, such as law enforcement officers, psychologists, and even case managers. She might have said how kind you were to her and that she never forgot you." They both sighed.

"Here are the Nike gym shoes and six pairs of socks to give to Angel. I didn't wrap them in case you need them to be examined for drugs. I thought I would be cautious," Rosie handed the shoe box to Daisy. "Thanks for providing them to Angel for me, Daisy."

"It wasn't required to be unwrapped since they will be provided to her by staff. I will wrap them, so she has something special to open for Christmas."

I will take you to the visitation room, now. If you would like to stop back, I will be here until at least three o'clock this afternoon. I can answer any questions you may have after your visit."

Rosie took a quick sip of her coffee and stood. Daisy opened her office door and the two of them walked side by side down the corridor.

They walked through the courtyard, on a narrow pavement, with an overhead aluminum covering. It wouldn't protect anyone from the wind, but it did keep them from being drenched by rain or snow. They entered a large auditorium and stopped to check in with the visitation officer. He searched Rosie's purse and returned it. As Rosie stood there, she noticed a stage at one end of the room. Just below the stage, a photographer was set up with a backdrop that looked like a Florida beach. It had the appearance of palm trees and water.

"You chose the right day to come, Rosie. The photographer isn't here every day. His schedule varies from week to week. He will provide you and Angel with a copy of a picture of the two of you. It is paid for by a local Christian organization."

"That sounds great. I would be glad to make a donation."

"Oh, no. It isn't necessary." Daisy led Rosie to a small, rectangular table positioned in a row of similar tables and chairs. "Angel should arrive momentarily. You two enjoy your lunch and getting acquainted." Daisy nodded at the visitation officer and left as Rosie sat down facing the door and put her purse on the floor between her feet.

Angel appeared in the doorway wearing her orange jumpsuit and black flipflops without socks. The visitation officer had her sign the log and pointed toward Dr. Rosie. Angel glanced over, flipped her hair back, and quickly approached Rosie. She smiled as she sat down on a rather cold metal chair, across from her guest.

"Hi, Dr. Rosie. I can't thank you enough for coming all this way." Angel clasped her hands together, smiled, and sat down across from Rosie.

"I am so pleased to meet you at last, Angel."

"You probably didn't recognize me. I had sandy brown hair until last week. I splurged and it included a shampoo." Angel sounded excited and fluffed her short, black hair."

"It looks great. Do you mind if I ask you what it cost you to splurge?"

"Nine dollars," Angel smiled and responded quickly.

Rosie didn't even attempt to stifle a laugh. She explained," that wouldn't even buy the dye today, Angel. Good for you."

Angel laughed too. And said, "I know we have shared a lot about ourselves in emails and in our telephone conversation. I have so much more to say now that you are here in person. I don't trust anyone in this reformatory. I take that back. I trust Chaplain Caroline, Mrs. Marigold and our medic, Dr. Jo. She doesn't just treat your symptoms. She listens and cares about me."

"I understand, Angel. Do you have something specific in mind?"

"I am so upset, Dr. Rosie. Angel lowered her voice and continued. My two surviving co-defendants, Song and James, get to have parole hearings. I just found out that a law was passed saying if a juvenile is sentenced to life without parole, they are entitled to parole hearings. I doubt that any of us could get released. The Toledo community thinks we are monsters and would publicly object. At least the two of them get to be heard and I can never be heard. I think that isn't fair. Not that I deserve it."

"Surviving co-defendants?"

"Yes. Marcus was executed. That leaves the three of us. James, Song, and I received the same life sentences. Unbelievable that I took the plea agreement when I didn't shoot anyone."

"You feel as though you are as deserving as them, if not more, right?"

"Well, at least I have been rehabilitated, so to speak. I can say that to a parole board. Isn't that what prison is supposed to be about? Or is it just to punish and make communities safer?"

"You have a point, Angel. I am so sorry. I see why this law makes you frustrated and angry.

I'm trying to locate your younger brothers, Greg and Mark Kessler, and your sister, Amanda Howard. Did you know I interviewed them when I was evaluating you for trial?"

"No. I mean, I don't remember if you told me because I've forgotten our times together in the County Jail. Why are you looking for them?"

"In the event that you ever have a hearing, they can testify to the details you share about your abusive childhood. That is something parole boards need to hear from first-hand witnesses."

"Oh. That is really nice of you. Does that mean you think somehow, I could have a hearing?"

"I will see what I can do with the assistance of several other professionals who are interested in you. No guarantees, of course."

"Wow. It gives me something to pray about, for sure."

"You've been told your brothers were adopted and had a loving Christian upbringing and great educations, right?"

"No. My grandmother is my mom's mom. She hasn't stayed connected with my half-brothers. We had different fathers. They were Rossi's kids and he treated them like little princes, but me like Cinderella, or worse. I do remember that my sister, Amanda, spent most weekends with her paternal grandparents. They had rights and my mother couldn't keep Amanda from them. By the time she turned twelve, she lived with them full-time. The law said you could choose who to live with at twelve. That is, if someone wanted you. It felt like nobody cared about me." Angel looked away. She took a deep breath and faced Rosie.

"I was nine, Dr. Rosie," Angel's voice quaked. "Once Amanda wasn't there to share a bedroom with me, Rossi was able to molest me. I don't know if he abused my sister. My mom never believed it. I think she was probably molested by her own father and that is why grandma divorced him."

"That's terrible, Angel. I am so very sorry." Not to be observed by the officer in charge, Rosie reached across the table and quickly patted Angel's hands."

"I never knew my father and I don't know if my mother knows who he is. My grandmother has no clue. She wasn't involved with us at that time. Rossi pretty much prevented my mother and me from being in touch with her."

"That is not uncommon, Angel. Abusers alienate the victims from outside supportive relationships and keep them totally dependent on them."

"You know the whole story about my mom running to Indiana to keep the family services people from taking us away."

"Yes, I heard that from your brothers when I first interviewed them."

Angel went on to explain, "After Rossi went to prison, mom divorced him. Then we lived in Indiana with Mom's next husband, Roger, along with Roger's parents, and younger brother, Buster. It was a two-bedroom house with an outhouse. I stunk and had to get on a yellow bus to go to school. My clothes were a mess. My shoes had holes. It was very embarrassing."

Angel's voice was barely above a whisper. "My life went from bad to worse. I was raped and pregnant by the age of thirteen. I am pretty sure Roger was the sperm daddy. He wasn't the only one who abused me." Angel's voice quivered. She bent her head down, clasped her hands together, and bit her lip hard.

"When we were all sent outdoors so Roger and my mom could have their privacy, the little boys would run off together and Buster would pull me by my hair, into the woods and molest me. Roger raped me when Mom went twice a month to the store. When I was thirteen, he took me to Columbus for an abortion. He told my mom he was taking the boys and me fishing. I can't believe she believed his story since he never took us anywhere for fun. Well, he signed me into the clinic and gave a phony address. He took my brothers fishing, all right. He picked me back up and supposedly nobody in the family knew anything or they ignored us like they always did. Dr. Klein, I get so angry when I think of that time in my life. I didn't know what to do, so I ran."

"The school counselor became suspicious. She asked me about my brothers. To avoid an investigation as to why they weren't in school, Roger moved us to his friends' house in the city. It was a druggie haven. I eventually quit school and ran away, back to Ohio."

"Angel, I am so sorry." Rosie started to reach for Angel's hands. This time she spotted a visitation officer heading toward them. She remembered the rule of no touching the inmates. She sat back in her chair and crossed her arms.

Their conversation was halted when a horn blew. Their food, and that of the other visitors, mostly women with children, was wheeled into the room by a food preparation employee.

Rosie wondered how much longer the other women inmates will be incarcerated, and I wonder how many of the little children belong to them. Most of the women visiting with the kids appear to be middle age, possibly their grandmothers. Well, I guess they could be social workers. What do these children know about why their mothers are sitting here in orange uniforms? How sad.

Rosie's thoughts were broken when their individual pepperoni pizzas with tater tots and cookies were placed in front of them. Rosie's attention returned to Angel and their lunches. "Would you like something to drink, Angel?"

"Yes, thank you. A diet coke would be great."

Rosie got up and approached the vending machines. She slipped the card she had purchased into the slot and punched the number associated with diet coke. A can came out. Rosie hit the number again, and another can dropped into the tray. She noticed the candy machine beside the drink machine. She placed her card into the slot and punched the number for Peanut M&M's. The little package dropped into the tray. She took the drinks and candy back to the table where Angel sat.

"Thank you," Angel said.

"Do you think it is okay, Angel, if we give the kids my cookies? They are wrapped individually in cellophane."

"I don't know Dr. Rosie. I haven't had a visitor in years. I don't know the rules other than that inmates aren't allowed to touch the vending machines or hug visitors." Angel took a bite of her pizza and wiped her chin with her napkin. She handed her cookies to Rosie and said, "I don't need these either."

Rosie pushed her chair back from the table and stood up. She walked toward the table with the visiting children and handed the cookies to one of the two women seated beside the kids. At first the younger woman appeared startled. Then she said thank you and smiled. She passed the cookies to the kids. The other older, grey-haired, woman stared ahead at the inmate they were visiting. The two kids looked alike. Maybe brother and sister, four and five years old. They said thank you, too. Rosie noticed they wore no socks, and their jeans were a size too small. *It is terribly cold out, she thought.*

Angel and Rosie shared the Peanut M&Ms, gulped down their drinks, and quickly finished their lunches. Angel asked, "Did you notice the photographer standing by the stage?"

"As a matter of fact, I did. Mrs. Marigold explained that he would take our picture together. Would you like that?"

"Sure. If you do. Then I can remember our visit and the color of my hair, since I probably won't have it dyed again," Angel said matter of factly.

"You saved your sewing income to do that, right?"

"Yes. It took my commissary account down to practically nothing."

Rosie thought I will definitely replenish Angel's account on-line when I get home.

They rose from their chairs and walked toward the stage. There was no longer a line, as there had been before lunch. The photographer smiled and positioned them in front of the Florida scene. Rosie put her arm around Angel's waist and Angel leaned her head toward Rosie's shoulder and smiled.

"Smile," he said. His instamatic produced two copies in color. He handed them to Rosie and Angel.

"Thank you very much, Bill," Rosie said. She was surprised that Angel knew the photographer's name. He wore no name tag.

"You know him, personally, Angel?"

"He videos our praise dance productions at Christmas and Easter. Bill is a very nice man."

Rosie thought it would be good to leave on a high note. "I will be leaving now," she said. " Let's talk on the phone next Friday if that works for you."

"It does. I am not working in the afternoon, so I can call earlier than the other women. They line up to make their calls around four o'clock. Does two or three o'clock work for you, Rosie?"

"Yes. I will make it work. I will put our little picture in a frame and place it on my desk in my home office. That is more private than having it displayed at work."

"At least we got a hug in because of taking our picture. Thank you so much for coming. Stay safe and don't catch a cold out there in the weather." Angel placed her hands together as though she was praying. Rosie did the same and gave a little bow.

She signed out of the visitation area and began strolling quickly through the courtyard to return to the front where she could retrieve her driver's license. Rosie noticed that Daisy's office door was closed. She decided not to stop. She was eager to call Bucky and get on the road. The sky looked unusually dark for mid-afternoon, and the country roads could become snowy or slick.

CHAPTER SEVEN

Reuniting with Stella

"Gump Law Office. This is Stella. How can I help you?"

"Hi roomie. It's me, Rosie. I was hoping to talk to the owner of your law firm and the love of your life, Travis. How are you?"

"I'm great. I'm filling in for our receptionist. She's on a well-earned vacation until after New Years. How are you? I was so sorry you had to miss our Adrian College homecoming reunion this past September. Even though you were only at Adrian a year, you would have known some of our classmates, and sorority sisters. How are you both?"

"We're fine. Bucky and I moved out into the country and enjoyed the beautiful Autumn colors. We don't even mind the snow, although driving to and from the offices and university may turn out to be a hassle."

"Travis isn't available this week. He has business in Naples, Florida. I might be able to connect you with our son, Devon. He is a Junior Law Partner now and Travis is basically retired."

"Tell Devon I said congratulations, but I can wait till Travis returns. I want to pick his brain about an old case. Will the two of you be available to have dinner with us between Christmas and New Years? We are coming down to Dayton to visit my mother and stepfather, Caleb."

"Sure. You can stay with us. Are they still enjoying life? Your mom must be in her upper 80's, right?"

"They sold their house and reside in an independent living facility. Staying with you will work. Thank you. Get this Stella, Mom and Caleb sailed across the Atlantic on the Queen Mary this past summer. Get this, they took ballroom dancing beforehand. The ship has an orchestra and several formal dances. In the Spring, they are planning a European river cruise. They have energy to spare."

"That's amazing. Tell you what, Rosie. I'll be talking to Travis tonight. His business is to check our condo so he can justify flying down to Florida to play three or four rounds of golf at the Naples Country Club." Stella laughed and then Rosie knew that her friend wasn't angry at her husband. "He can probably give you a call tomorrow after eighteen holes. Will you be available in the afternoon or are you working?"

"I will gladly take his call. I might kid him about the monkey business he is taking care of."

"Is your cell phone number still the same?"

"Yes. It is. I'll get back to you, Stella, with more details about our trip down to Dayton. Great talking to you and thank you for connecting me to your talented husband."

"Well, talented in some ways and just plain stubborn in others."

"Bye, Rosie. My other line is ringing. It could be Travis."

***

As she hung up her cell phone, Rosie's Summerhill office phone was ringing. Ruth was off for chorus practice. She sang with a local group of women and the Christmas season meant a lot of practice for numerous engagements. Clubs and residential facilities enjoyed listening to their renditions of popular Christmas carols.

"Hello, Dr. Klein. This is Sheriff Holland. I would like to bring you up to date on the poisoning of your dog, Champ."

"Oh, thank you for calling, Sheriff Holland."

"We identified a suspect. He had a limp and was trying to jump a fence at your old condo complex in Sylvania Ohio. The owners had a visual security system. Apparently, their automatic lights came on, their dog barked, and the guy got scared and ran. The camera caught him before he could turn his back to the door. Although they were not home, the woman, Mrs. Palmer, saw the entire thing on her cell phone and notified the police. I'd like to stop by so you can look at the video and a photo spread. We need to see if you recognize the guy pictured. He was wearing a black hoodie and black leather gloves. All the men in the photos will have on hoodies. He carried a plastic grocery bag. We don't know what was in it. We aren't sure of his race, possibly Hispanic."

"Well, I will see what I can do. You said his face was not visible?"

34

"No, but although he escaped by running, he had a noticeable limp. Maybe his size and that factor will assist you in recognizing him."

"Do you want to come all the way out here, or do you prefer that I come into the precinct?"

"Deputy Burkhard and I will come out and take another look around the chain linked perimeter of the property and the front gate. Since it happened before the snow fell, possibly his shoes or boots left imprints in the soft soil and are covered by the snow."

"We had to be home, at least one of us, for Champ to be loose. He never used to be allowed out without a leash. Our homeowner's association had strict rules about that. Now, we have fenced in three of our ten acres. We thought it was perfectly safe to let him out alone."

"I would have thought so, too, Dr. Klein. The crime against you was not random. We don't know whether the two crimes are related to the same perpetrator. We need to interview you to see if there is anyone you can think of who has posed a threat to you, in any way. This could be just revenge, or it could be a warning."

"When can you come? The sooner the better when you put it that way. Meanwhile I will talk to Bucky and put my thinking cap on. I have evaluated many disgruntled clients over the course of my career."

Rosie had just seen Bucky come in the side kitchen door from the garage. She was positioned on a stool at the kitchen island and beckoned him over.

"I couldn't help but overhear your end of the conversation. Was that the Sheriff? What's going on Rosie?" Bucky asked. as he massaged her shoulders from behind and planted a kiss at the base of her neck.

Rosie swiveled around, looked up at Bucky with a smile, and said, "That was Sheriff Holland. He's coming out with his deputy to look around the property and ask me questions about potential suspects and their motives."

"Really?' Do they have a lead?"

"They have a photo spread for me to look at and a video of a guy attempting to break into a condo, quite near to where we used to live. Sheriff Holland wants to know if anyone has threatened me. They think our dog being poisoned was definitely not a random act."

"Geez, Rosie. That's scary." Bucky took her hand and led her to the loveseat in the family room.

"Sheriff Holland has two different motives in mind. One is that it is meant to be revenge. The other is that it's a warning."

Rosie's voice faded as her mind became preoccupied with the idea that her life could be in danger.

"Don't worry, Rosie. We'll put our heads together and figure it out. Sounds like the authorities are on top of it."

CHAPTER EIGHT

The Call from Travis

"Hi Travis. Thank you for returning my call so promptly."

"You're welcome, Rosie. How's Bucky?"

"Bucky's fine. Busy with recruitment for next year's basketball and football teams. Fall sports at the University always involve his participation with the coaches and players. You and Stella should come up for a basketball game this winter. We have lovely guest quarters now, above the garage. We moved to the country you know. We can take you cross country skiing."

"Maybe we will do just that. Stella has a cute little snow suit she rarely has occasion to wear. So, how can I be of assistance, Rosie?"

"Here's the situation. I've befriended an inmate at the Ohio Reformatory for Women. She is in prison for life. I don't remember if I ever told you about her. Her name is Angel Morgan."

"I think you might have discussed her with Stella. She didn't provide me with any details, but she mentioned that you have become very interested in this woman's case."

"True, I find her to be remorseful and helpful to other inmates by telling them her story. I won't go into it all now. Basically, I was hoping you could look at the research I've completed and my evaluation of her for Court. I'd like an expert legal opinion. She has been sentenced to life without parole, never held a gun, and testified as State's witness against the shooters. The guys killed six people."

"How did you come to know her so well?"

"I was appointed to evaluate her for Competency to Stand Trial. Then she accepted a deal instead of going to trial. It upset me. She was on my mind through the years. I finally made written contact. We have had an email relationship. Happy to say, I recently visited her for the first time. I plan to go back."

"I'd be glad to look over your materials. Have you thought about writing to Governor Stanley to intervene in her case? Stella and I just spent time with him and his wife, Jan."

"Really?" Rosie responded in a very surprised tone.

"Yes, it was a sad occasion. My brother-in-law passed away. He had been an advocate for a prisoner and visited him once a month for years. It came to Governor Stanley's attention. He and his wife quietly attended the memorial service last month. The media was unaware. His security team fit right in with the mourners in their dark suits. Governor Stanley didn't do it to impress voters even though his re-election comes up next year. He is just a good, Godly man."

"My friend, Agent Ron Thompson of the FBI, and a local Toledo newspaper journalist, Wes Hall have encouraged me to pursue the idea of having her sentence commuted by the Governor. I am not saying she was a nice girl, but the abuse she suffered through her childhood contributed to her attitudes and immoral, illegal behavior and the system failed her. Maybe when you get up here, we can meet with Ron and Wes, and they can pick your brain as to how to assist her."

"I'd enjoy that, Rosie. Did you say Thompson is now an FBI agent?"

"Yes. He was the State Highway Patrolman who arrested Angel during the time of the crime spree. He was promoted to the FBI after a lengthy career in state law enforcement."

"We will make plans as soon as I get back from Naples. I do hate leaving this weather. If we didn't have close family to spend Christmas with, Stella and I might have considered staying here over the holidays. She is busy at home. She bakes cookies and wraps gifts, of course."

"Are you playing golf tomorrow?"

"Funny you should ask. Last round before I fly home later in the day." Travis laughed.

"Hit them long and straight. Stay safe as Angel always says to me. Merry Christmas, Travis."

"Merry Christmas, Rosie. Stella and I will look forward to your visit and to coming up to Summerhill and seeing a basketball game in January."

CHAPTER NINE

The Meeting

As Rosie entered the Embassy Restaurant, she could see Wes Hall, the Toledo Blade journalist, and Ron Thompson sitting across from one another at a booth in the back of the narrow aisle. She stepped ahead of other customers waiting to be seated, apologized to them, and quickly approached her colleagues.

"So nice to see you again, Wes. Glad that Ron arranged our lunch." Ron moved over and Rosie slid in beside him.

Conversation was interrupted when the handsome young server handed them menus and asked for their drink orders. Even though it was a pub, they simply ordered water and black coffee.

"Good to see you, too, Rosie. You haven't aged a bit. That marriage must be working well."

"Yes, Wes. Bucky is a great husband."

"He's still at the University, right?" Wes asked.

"Not exactly. Not permanently. He retired but is back. Long story. He loves his job as Interim Athletic Director. He still enjoys recruiting young men and women for various sports."

"Sharon and I have seasons tickets for basketball, and we can see him up in the announcer's box. Where do you sit, Rosie?" Ron asked.

"When Bucky isn't being interviewed by the announcers, we sometimes are invited to sit in the President's private box. Otherwise, I sit three rows above the home bench, mid-court, and bring a friend to fill in Bucky's reserved seat."

"I heard a rumor that your allegiance to the University of Toledo goes back to your undergraduate days. Is that true?"

"You could say that. I received three degrees from the University. One was in Physical Education, and the next was a M.Ed. in Counseling, and finally a Ph.D. The faculty in the College of Education were very supportive of me."

"Wow. How so?" Ron asked.

The server placed their drinks down and removed himself, seeing the three customers were engrossed in conversation and not ready to order yet.

"To tell you the truth, I was not a scholarly undergraduate student. I was a cheerful, bubbly, basketball half time dancer, in the group known as the university dancing Rockettes.

Ron was taking a gulp of his coffee. Rosie's comment nearly caused him to spit it out. He and Wes laughed at Rosie's description of herself.

"How did dancing enable you to go through grad school? Did you teach it?" Wes asked.

"No. The education professors liked me because on Mondays, in their classes, they could talk to me about the weekend basketball game. The chairman of the counselor education department invited me to participate in a yearlong master's degree program, and later to go through a Ph.D. program. Both were all expenses paid. I was blessed."

"That's amazing, Rosie." Ron glanced at Wes who was nodding his head in agreement.

The server returned to take their orders. The Greek chicken/rice-lemon soup, and Greek salad appealed to Rosie, while the guys chose soup and half of a BLT.

Once their plates were removed and dessert was declined, their conversation took on a more serious tone. Rosie began discussing Angel's circumstances. Wes needed to be brought up to date.

"I researched the legal processes for an appeal of sentences and ways to overturn a sentence. From what I could tell, those options are not available for a "lifer" who took a plea deal and has served a couple decades. The statute of limitation has long since passed. The only thing remotely possible is to have her sentence commuted by our Governor." Rosie explained.

"That's a great idea, Rosie. Maybe he would commute it with time served. After all, it has been more than twenty-five years, hasn't it? Or maybe she could get out on parole?" Ron asked.

Their checks arrived. Ron grabbed all three and announced, "Holiday gifts, my pleasure."

Rosie looked at Wes and he shrugged his shoulders. "Thank you," Wes said.

Rosie remembered to grab her jacket and gloves from the booth. She lost her red jacket the last time she ate there. The three walked out into a brisk, cold, but sunny afternoon.

CHAPTER TEN

Mail from Angel

Hi Dr. Rosie,

I can't begin to tell you what it meant to me that you took the time to visit me. Please thank your husband. I'm sorry I couldn't meet him in person. I wonder if I am picturing him right. Is he six feet tall? Dark or light hair? Thin or with muscles? I know he loves you a lot. I will never have love like that.

I know you are both very busy with your jobs and your moving to the country. I am sorry to hear about your dog, Champ. Do you really think someone poisoned him? That is just horrible. I wish I had a cat, too. I can't believe a cat would ever cuddle with me at night.

If I could give you a Christmas gift, I would send a special Christmas ornament for your first Christmas in your new home. I used to dream of having a little Christmas tree to decorate and my very own apartment.

You said that Bucky chops wood for the fireplace. In my mind's eye, I picture the two of you seated in front of a blazing fire, drinking hot chocolate with little marshmallows. Maybe with toast to dunk. Please describe it for me when you write. And tell Bucky to be careful chopping that wood.

In my journal that you gave me, I wrote about your visit. I have our picture together taped to the inside of the cover. Every night before I go to sleep, I write a prayer of gratitude for your friendship.

Well, I need to take a shower. I feel yucky from working seven hours today. We will be off until New Years. That is good and bad. Good that my old body gets a rest. Bad that I won't make money and the time will go very slowly. They let us play games and read books and Bibles. We will probably have a couple chapel services. I hate being bored more than I dislike aching muscles.

I will be thinking of you. Be safe and stay well. Love ya,
Angel

CHAPTER ELEVEN

Collect Call

"Ohio Reformatory for Women calling Dr. Rosie Klein. Will you accept a collect call from inmate Angel Morgan?"

"Yes," Rosie said without hesitation.

"Hi Dr. Rosie. How are you? I've been trying to call but my calls are rejected. I was worried."

"I am fine, Angel. Your calls weren't identified. Sorry. I am very glad to hear from you."

"You won't believe this, Dr. Rosie. I talked to my grandma, and she said she heard from my sister, Amanda. My grandma has lived in the same house that she grew up in and never changed her land phone number. Amanda will be coming through Toledo on the way to Windsor, Canada. She wants to see Grandma. She will be alone. I guess it is some kind of business trip. Grandma asked her to stay overnight. Amanda said she might be able to do that. I can't wait. Maybe we can talk on the phone. Wouldn't that be wonderful, Dr. Rosie? She is probably about fifty years old. She could be a grandma, herself by now."

"That sounds great, Angel. I'm sure you missed your big sister, Amanda, a lot when she moved to her grandparents."

"More than you could ever know for lots of reasons. For one thing, I have never told anyone. I was jealous that she escaped our stepfather's abuse." In a very soft voice, Angel said, "Don't get me wrong. I loved my sister.

I have prayed to hear the voices of my sister and brothers again. I know I will never be able to see them, but to talk and get to know them as grown-ups would be a dream come true. The fact that they would be willing to talk to a convict like me, is a miracle."

"I understand your mixed feelings, Angel. That is normal for anyone in your circumstances. I am happy for you. I remember from talking to your brothers that they held nothing against you. They understood how you fell into the friendships with the little group. They recall your childhood and all the abuse you took from their father, their stepfather, and your mother. They have no contact with your mother and desire none. They thought at the time that she might still have been in prison, and they were grateful she would not be serving time in your facility."

"What will you do on Christmas, Angel?" Rosie asked, hoping to change the subject to something more cheerful. Although on second thought, being incarcerated on Christmas, year after year, could be depressing.

Angel said, "Other than opening your package and a Christmas stocking filled with donations from a local church, not much. We will have a turkey dinner with the usual sides. I was told the stocking will have cookies, nutrition bars, Raman noodles, cocoa, mints, gum, a puzzle book, a pencil with sharpener, a deck of cards, rubber bands for your hair, but mine is too short. Oh, and the chaplains will provide a Woman's Devotional with room for journaling. I feel blessed this year. Mostly, because I got to see you and we have a picture of each other. But getting a stocking and journal is definitely a nice surprise. I am pretty sure Chaplain Caroline had a lot to do with it."

"First time ever?"

"Yup. As a kid, my mother never hung stockings or let us think there was a Santa Claus, let alone a baby Jesus. If it wasn't for the church down the street on Wednesday nights, I would not have known anything about God's existence or love for little children. My mother never even missed us on Wednesday nights. They fed us at church. I also always wondered if that pastor asked about what happened to us. We moved in the middle of the night after Rossi was arrested."

"In one of our interviews at the Lucas County Jail, you told me about going to that church after school on Wednesdays. Their bus picked you up at school, right?"

"Yes. How can you remember things about me from so long ago? You must have had zillions of cases in all these years. Are you in touch with any other prisoners?"

"No. I am not in contact much with other women inmates. You stood out, Angel. What you have accomplished through these years is amazing. It seems like you don't have a lazy bone in your body, and you are very inquisitive. Do you know what that means?"

"I think so. It means I am not lazy. Anyone will tell you I am a hard worker in the sewing workshop. I have had no trouble with my supervisors. Hmm? Inquisitive. Does that mean curious?"

"Yes. It does. It drives you to learn new things and maybe find out more about old things."

"That's for sure. I need to change what I said. The first ten years, I was not accepted to work in the sewing workshop. I had too many reprimands for my temper, didn't listen to directions, ignored rules, and stuff like that. You have to qualify to work and make a little money."

"You have made up for those years. Now, assistant supervisor. You mentioned that Chaplain Caroline helped turn your attitude around. How did that happen?"

"She asked me to attend Celebrate Recovery which is an addiction recovery group. It can be any addiction, not just drugs or alcohol. It is a Christian twelve step program like AA. You know, Alcoholics Anonymous. AA refers to a higher power, but not specifically to God and Jesus. Once I passed the step of making amends for my sins toward others, my mind and emotions settled down. Before that, I blamed everyone else, and I was told that he was feeling entitled. When I didn't get what I thought I wanted, I pouted, withdrew, or acted out by punching someone or the wall."

"That must have been a dreadful time. I can see why you felt the way you did. Like you said, it was amazing how you turned your life around. Thank you for sharing that journey with me. I want you to know that you can tell me anything, Angel. I look forward to hearing more about your life and your feelings. Would you like to talk again soon?"

"Oh, yes. I am glad I didn't turn you away with my nasty story."

"Of course, not, Angel. Call me on the day after New Years. Maybe we can set some goals for both of us for the year. What do you think of that?"

"That would be a great idea. I need goals and deadlines. It gives me hope and patience."

"Okay, Angel. Talk to you on January 2, about five o'clock, if it works for you."

"I can make it work, Dr. Rosie. Happy New Year. Stay safe and well."

"And you, Angel. Thank you again for calling. Bye."

CHAPTER TWELVE

The Photo Spread

"Good evening, Dr. Klein. Deputy Burkhard, who you met, is on vacation. This is Agent Liza Cunningham of the F.B.I. We are working together because we think the people who poisoned your dog served time for crimes committed in more than one State."

"Hi Agent Cunningham. I remember when you were Ron Thompson's rookie partner."

"Yes. Just call me Liza."

"That goes for me, too. Well, not Liza, but call me Thadd," Sheriff Holland laughed, as did the women.

Rosie chimed in. "I am simply Rosie."

Agent Cunningham replied to Rosie's comment about her being Agent Thompson's rookie. "Oh, yes. And he was quite the trainer, I must say. Stern, professional, very knowledgeable, and determined to make me the best agent possible. Good to see you again. Sorry it is under these circumstances."

"Thank you both for stopping by. You can place your hats and overcoats on the bench." Rosie pointed to a small oak bench positioned just inside the front door beneath a wooden row of pegs. Her scarf hung on a peg, her black leather driving gloves were folded on the bench, and her rubber boots were positioned beneath it.

"Would you like a hot beverage on this cold winter evening? I have cocoa, coffee, tea?"

"Thank you," said Thadd. "I have the twelve-hour graveyard shift and black coffee sounds good."

Liza followed suit by asking for the same. Rosie returned with four steaming mugs of coffee and placed them on the coffee table in front of Thadd and Liza along with a small, decorative plate of hot chocolate chip cookies. Bucky entered the family room and introduced himself. He and Rosie sat down in wing back chairs across from the law enforcement couple. No sooner were they seated than Willow hopped into Bucky's lap.

"Daddy's girl?" asked Liza.

"You might say so." Rosie leaned toward Bucky and scratched Willow's head.

"Here's what we have so far, Rosie. It appears that a sister-brother couple are very interested in paying you back for causing them to serve time in a Michigan State Prison for a lengthy stint. Their names are Bonnie and Clyde Tipton. Sound familiar?"

"Of course. They were grabbing young girls for sex trafficking. How could I ever forget? I know you said they spent a long time, but how did they ever get out? And didn't the FBI arrest them? Their crime spree crossed state lines."

"Good question. They turned state's witness against the Chinese mafia, on behalf of the Feds. It was determined that the State's case was primary due to the fact they were arrested in Michigan and housed there. They were permitted to serve the sentences concurrently because with their testimonies the Feds were able to bust the Chinese ring leaders. However, they are out on parole which means if they violate the terms of parole, they go back for another ten years."

"How did they find Rosie's country home and how seriously do they want to injure her?" Bucky asked.

"It seems that Bonnie Tipton politely asked the parking attendant at the LaSalle Tower if Dr. Klein still maintained an office there. He said yes, on Fridays. They waited till that Friday and followed you home, Rosie. They were in her brother Clyde's old black Nissan. which was less noticeable than Bonnie's cute, little, blue BMW convertible. They passed by your house when you turned into the driveway and watched you use your remote control to open the gate."

"Wow. If I had met Bucky for dinner somewhere, it would have made it more difficult for them to remain out of sight, wouldn't it or even known where we live," Rosie said.

"Probably so. They had already been watching the Summerhill office. Security caught sight of the Nissan in Zink's meat market parking lot across the street from your building. It was a Monday, and the market was closed. The license plate is from Michigan, not Ohio this time. They are probably required not to leave the state. That alone violates their parole, "Sheriff Holland said.

"And, of course, they aren't permitted to have weapons or alcohol on them or in their vehicle," Agent Cunningham added.

"What happens next?" Rosie asked.

"We can't prove they poisoned your dog yet. We need to wait for their next move. We have the address of the apartment they share in Troy Michigan. It is a large, three-story house converted into seven apartments. They rented the entire left side of the first floor. That way they have a front and back exit to avoid possible law enforcement. And their windows on the side are low enough to jump down to the driveway where their vehicles are parked," Thadd explained.

"Interestingly, there was a house of prostitution nearby at the time the traffickers were arrested twenty some years ago. Back then, the kidnapped girls were housed at a Red Roof Inn, with no transportation, money, cell phones, or identification. They slept days, six to a room. Their pimps paid the girls' motel rent by the week and shot them up with heroin to keep them dependent. They serviced men in massage parlors, residences, hotels, and casinos. The pimps lived together in a decent, four-bedroom, suburban home near Troy Athens High School."

"Liza spoke to the wardens at both their state prisons and found out that Clyde was released about nine months after Bonnie. She had to provide an address and her means of transportation. Clyde was required to live with a relative and provide his parole officer with his means of transportation. They have no other relatives maintaining a relationship with them," Sheriff Holland said.

"I am stunned. I had no idea when they kidnapped Alexis Pappas and then tried to grab Megan and Madison Small, that it was such a vast system," Rosie said. Bucky reached over and rubbed her shoulder.

"As sex offenders both Clyde and Bonnie had to register their addresses for the community to be aware of them and their offenses. I believe the Detroit Free Press got ahold of their release dates. They published small articles about them in the local section, and in the weekly Troy Times," Agent Cunningham said.

"The Chinese men certainly knew what they were doing. They researched the area. Troy is ranked number one as the safest city in Michigan. It is twenty- two miles North of Detroit where it is assumed that most crime occurs. No one would suspect a trafficking ring to be housed in and operating from that suburb," Sheriff Holland added.

"We don't need to show you a photo spread now that we have the suspects. But you might want to look at their current appearance. Here are their mug shots when they were booked many years ago and a couple pictures that our surveillance team took when they were staking out your offices." Liza handed the photos to Rosie and Bucky leaned toward her to look at them too.

"They haven't aged well, have they?" Bucky commented to the three of them.

"Well, I remembered her as a red head and now she has short cropped gray hair. I don't remember much about Clyde, but he looks a little stoop shouldered and that was definitely not part of his appearance at the school. You said he has a limp. Now that you mention it, I do remember that the security guard at the school walked through the halls with a limp," said Rosie.

"How will you ever be able to get a search warrant for their apartment and vehicles?" Bucky asked in a very concerned voice.

"That's an excellent question, Bucky. We need probable cause do that. If they are pulled over for a minor traffic violation and there happen to be drugs or weapons in the car, we might be able to convince a Judge to let us search. That would be a violation of their parole. Even a busted taillight or burned-out headlight would do it. It wouldn't have to be a moving violation," explained Sheriff Holland.

Rosie smiled. Her eyebrows raised and a mischievous look came over her face. *Hmm? A busted taillight? She thought. Maybe I should start carrying a baseball bat in my car. For protection purposes.* She smiled again.

Liza spoke up. "Don't even think it, Rosie. Whatever it is, won't work." All four of them laughed.

"Okay. But don't you think I should keep a baseball bat on the front seat for protection? I'm serious."

"No. It doesn't stand up well against a gun directed at you through the driver's window. I would advise you not to pump gas without me. Watch your rear-view mirror, Rosie. Carry your keys in your hand so you can hit the emergency button and basically be cautious and observant of your immediate surroundings," said Bucky.

"How about a Glock, Bucky?" Rosie asked. I've heard that it is quite light, cheaper than other models, and reliable."

"I don't advise her to carry a gun, do you Sheriff?" Bucky asked.

Agent Cunningham and Sheriff Holland stood up, followed by Rosie. Bucky put Willow down and joined them as they walked toward the foyer.

"We will stay in touch. I might add. If you are dining out, ask for bottled water for a while. Or order a bottle of wine, rather than a glass. We don't know if poisoning is going to be their modus operandi. Less visible than a gun or knife," said Liza.

"That's a great suggestion. Thank you," said Bucky.

Rosie opened the front door and the law enforcement duo stepped out. A light snow was falling that brightened the otherwise long, dark driveway. Bucky double bolted it and left the front light on. He walked to the back of the house and turned on the patio lights. "Might as well light up the night, as they say," Bucky said as he tried to lessen Rosie's anxiety.

"Let's have that bottle of wine now, Bucky. I am hungry. Are you?"

Although Bucky had lost his appetite from the story the Agent and Sheriff had shared with them, he tried to appear cheerful for Rosie's sake. "Yes, Precious. I am."

"Well, then let's enjoy the rest of our evening and trust that law enforcement will protect us and hold Tipton's accountable for the death of our sweet dog, Champ, at the very least."

CHAPTER THIRTEEN

A Look Back in Time

Lying on her bunk, waiting for the call to supper, Angel felt incredibly grateful for the relationships she formed in the past few years. First, there was Chaplain Caroline, whose caring nature and encouraging words gave her hope and purpose. Angel didn't know where she would be, mentally and physically if it were not that her third case manager, Mrs. Marigold, connected her with Chaplain Caroline, who she learned to call Chappy. Maybe she'd be dead.

Angel came to realize that her body suffered when her mind and attitude were in the dumpster. Chappy taught her that God loves her; that He is her heavenly father, and that Jesus is truly her friend. Unconditional love, after all the ways she had screwed up her life and the lives of others, was an amazing thought. Undeserved, that's for sure and hard to believe.

Without a caring, earthly father, she felt so worthless. She questioned her very existence. How could she see Father God as loving and not punitive and harsh? Without a female role model, she failed to learn how to engage in nurturing relationships or take proper care of herself as a young woman. How could she ever function in society all alone? All she had known was rejection, anger, hate, and abuse. Learning to trust anyone took time. Too much time. She tended to do outrageous things. Her motives were to test the sincerity of others. When they refused to remain her friend, it confirmed her feelings of hopelessness. She harbored suicidal thoughts but had no plan. The doctors said she was not a danger to self or others.

Well, no doubt about it, she failed miserably outside these walls. With the structure in prison of three meals a day, a shower as needed, a bed and safe place to lay her head, she survived. It was one day at a time. Dr. Jo, the prison medic, prescribed blood pressure medications which allowed her to function well enough to go to work. Angel told Dr. Jo that she loves work. It makes the days go faster and makes her feel useful. By sewing the sides and bottom hems of dozens of flags, she could see the tangible results of her efforts. Some co-workers told her to slow down. She was making them look bad. Angel didn't fault them for being lazy. She simply took pride in her work.

Most days, after work she took a shower, changed uniforms, and rested. The hot water made her back and joints feel better. Arthritis of the spine, Dr. Jo diagnosed. No strong drugs permitted, just Ibuprofen or extra strength Tylenol.

On weekends, she enjoyed reading quietly in the prison library. She read newspapers to keep up to date on what was happening outside the walls. Reading usually took her mind off her pain and circumstances. While she felt she was doing fairly well, she still had bouts of depression that made it difficult for her to get up and face the day. Knowing this would be her routine forever, sometimes overwhelmed her. Church on Saturday evening and on Sunday morning gave her something to look forward to after the work week. Visiting Pastors preached messages that seemed as though they were communicating God's plans to her.

CHAPTER FOURTEEN

Three Classy Ladies

"That is nice of your roommate, Stella, to invite us to stay with them. Now that your mom and stepdad have sold their home and live in an independent senior living facility, staying with them is no longer an option. I guess we could stay at a nice motel, Precious."

"Stella would be offended if we turned down their invitation and stayed elsewhere. Besides, you really hit it off with Travis, didn't you? In terms of my parents, I think it is great that they don't feel obligated to stay within the confines of their new apartment. Some residents go nowhere because three meals a day are included in their monthly fees. Cruising and dancing will keep Mom and Caleb young and vibrant."

"We don't have to wait to retire completely, Rosie, to cruise and to dine and dance."

"I will take you up on that, Bucky. For now, let's have fun with friends and family on our little road trip. Too bad we have to leave Willow with Ruth particularly on a holiday weekend. I just don't want to risk causing anyone an allergic reaction like Ron Thompson had in my office."

" First of all, Willow doesn't know it is a holiday weekend. Secondly, Ruth told us she is happy to have the company of a feline. Lastly, it seems quite common for people to be allergic to cats. Having dogs all those years, it didn't occur to us that getting Willow would limit entertaining guests at home. Even putting Willow in another part of the house won't help. The dander also known as dead skin cells, remains with the furniture and our clothes, I believe," Bucky said.

"Yup. Did you know, Bucky, it even sticks to surfaces, not just furniture and carpets? And the fact that it is invisible to the human eye makes it more difficult to clean. They say that less clutter leaves the cat fewer objects to release dander. Aren't you proud that I researched all that?"

"Except that you didn't research it prior to adopting her from the shelter. Not that it would have mattered. You fell in love instantly. The foster parents said she was spade and had all her shots. Anyway, always proud of you, Precious. Don't tell me you think I like to accumulate stuff. My job requires me to keep records of recruits, athletes, and coaches."

"Bucky. That doesn't mean you need to leave them scattered all over the floor along with a zillion sports magazines. Willow adores you and is always perched as close to you as she can get. That means you are carrying the dander to everyone positioned around. So much for that subject. Would you please find some easy listening music?" Rosie asked.

Bucky quickly opened a bottle of Shiraz and poured two glasses. He put Rosie's on the kitchen island in front of her where she had prepared a platter of olives, cheese, and crackers for them. "Thank you, Bucky. I am thinking how enjoyable it will be to just hang out with Stella and Travis. I remember their son, Devon, when he was just a toddler. Now he is a junior partner in the Gump law firm."

"I hear an incoming call on our land line, Rosie. Want to get it, or should I? Bucky asked.

"I will get it," Rosie said as she sat her wine down and wiped her mouth.

"Hello, this is the Ohio Reformatory for Women with a collect call from Angel Morgan. Is the call accepted?"

"Yes," Rosie said. Strange, she thought. She and Angel weren't scheduled to talk until January. She hoped Angel was not calling with an emergency. Instantly Angel's voice came on the line. "Hi Dr. Rosie. It's me, Angel. Thank you for taking my call."

"What a pleasure, Angel. How are you?"

"To tell you the truth, not so well. I sort of needed to hear your voice if you don't mind. I have had the flu. It is spreading like wildfire. Someone must have brought it in, like visitors or staff. We are on quarantine again. It probably won't be the last time this winter. Talk about boring. I hate sitting on my bed or lying down all day long. Last week I had serious symptoms, like wanting to sleep all the time but not being able to rest because of a deep, constant cough. Dr. Jo gave me some cough medicine, Vitamin C chewables, Zinc tablets, and extra-strength Tylenol for my sore ribs and headache."

"I am so sorry, Angel. How long will you be quarantined?"

"Several church choirs are due to come in and entertain us next week. I think by then, most inmates will be non-contagious and symptom free. I love it when the churches take an interest in us and put on concerts with instruments. It brings back memories from my early childhood when I got to attend the little church down the street. That is, until my mom moved us in the middle of the night to avoid family interference, as she put it. It really was child protective services."

"I remember that you moved to Indiana at about nine years old, right?"

"Yes, and after that I don't remember celebrating Christmas or birthdays."

"I'm glad you called. I want to remind you that you can talk to me about anything, any time. If you need to call, feel free. At times I might be a little difficult to get ahold of. We are driving to my mother's. We will be seeing my college friends. He is a lawyer and is interested in your case."

"That sounds nice for a couple of reasons. First, that you have a neat relationship with your mother, and she welcomes you with open arms, no doubt. Second, that you have long-term close friendships. Oh, and that you have a lawyer friend who knows all about me. Thank you."

Their conversation was interrupted by a recorded message saying their allotted time was up. Thirty second warning. Rosie smiled to herself and thought it quite humorous that Angel numbered the points she wanted to make, just like Bucky does.

"Bye Dr. Rosie. I feel better just talking to you. Stay safe on your trip and don't get sick. It is not fun, especially when you are cold and alone."

"Take care of yourself, Angel. Take your medicine. Rest. Drink lots of liquid. You didn't mention Chaplain Caroline. Lean on her. She wants you to do that."

"Here's the problem. She is on vacation until the middle of January. She goes on a short-term mission trip each year at this time. It will be fun to hear all about it, but she isn't available now when I need her. Besides, she isn't allowed near us when we are in quarantine."

"Well, then, that is more reason why you should be calling me." The line went dead. Their conversation was abruptly discontinued.

"Bucky, I'm done talking to Angel." Rosie strolled into the family room carrying the cheese platter. Bucky was sitting with Willow in his lap, listening to recorded smooth jazz music. Two wine glasses and a bottle of Shiraz were sitting on the little table between the chairs.

"That was unexpected. Is everything alright?" Bucky asked.

"Yes and no. Angel has had the flu which puts her entire unit on quarantine. She is better but from her voice and conversation, I could tell she is feeling lonely and discouraged."

"It sounds like she really needs your support."

"That's what I was thinking, too.

"It is good that she is comfortable enough with your relationship to call, Rosie."

Rosie took a sip of wine and sat down beside Bucky. She answered, "I plan to call Chaplain Caroline and Dr. Jo to ask them to check on her and encourage her.:

"Great idea, Rosie."

CHAPTER FIFTEEN

Bonnie and Clyde

Bonnie returned to the apartment from Walmart with her arms full of grocery bags. She was lamenting about the cost of cigarettes and beer. She was cautious in the store that no one was watching her when she loaded the case of beer. She and her brother, Clyde, were not permitted to indulge in alcohol. Thankfully, cigarettes are permissible. Not that it would stop them, if they were not. Now that they were out of prison, old habits resurfaced easily.

Clyde was reclining on an old, weathered, green couch watching wrestling. Although he heard his sister come in, he didn't budge to help her carry in the groceries, beer, or cigarette cartons. He blamed his lame leg on preventing him from helping with household chores.

"Have you watched the news, Clyde?" Bonnie asked as she laid the groceries on the counter.

"Naw. I am not interested in politics or local crime. So, why would I watch the news?"

"Well, Dr. Rosie Klein, is quite notorious. You never know when she might appear at a press conference on the courthouse steps along with local law enforcement. That reporter, Wes, what's his name, is still poking around. He hasn't aged much, except for his receding forehead."

"Poking around? You don't think we were spotted poisoning the stupid dog, do you?"

"I don't see how. You quickly picked up the red jacket left behind by the wench at the Embassy Restaurant Pub and stuffed it into your LaSalle's Shopping bag. There were no security cameras in the restaurant, only out front and back. We're lucky her lunch dates at the Embassy are so predictable."

"You're right, Clyde. It was a stroke of luck that her jacket, hanging on the back of her chair while we were stalking her, caught your eyes. At least with our disguises, we were unrecognizable."

"Following her home was definitely easy, too. So many years have passed that it was unlikely she would have recognized my old Nissan from that elementary school parking lot. Being a security guard was really the key to picking up little girls, wasn't it? I am glad we waited a week to toss her bright red jacket, so it landed just outside the gate. Bonnie, do you realize how miserably cold I was when I tramped through the wet snow for at least a hundred yards to throw that stinking bag of raw meat between the bars of the front gate?"

"I know, brother. I wasn't very considerate of your comfort, was I?" Bonnie laughed and handed Clyde a lit Lucky Strike and a can of Corona Light.

Clyde popped the cap, took a gulp, and a drag of his cigarette, and continued. " When you pulled up to pick me up, there were no lights near the gate and the snow nearly blinded me. That means, their visibility from the house was nil."

"I think we pulled it off. The next step to end her career will require more specific planning to ensure we are not identified. Yes, because men and women in prison could recognize our mug shots on the television news."

"For sure, because I'm not going back to a stifling hot or freezing cold cell ever again.

If it weren't for her interference at the school, we would have been home scott free. Those little girls would never have been located and that Alex Pappas girl would have continued to make the Chinese lots of money. You did such a great job, Bonnie, gaining their trust so they would get into your car."

"They turned me down until that rainy day when I offered to take them to their mother's beauty shop. All along, the younger sister was eager to ride in my fancy little car. It was her skeptical big sister who protected them."

"I watched them carefully at school. You are right. The older one, Megan I think was her name, kind of watched as her sister walked down the hall to her classroom. Then she waited just outside the door when school got out."

"If it weren't for the fact that our little sister, Cindy, served time with Angel Morgan and commented that she was at Marysville, we most likely would have lost track of Klein. It seems that Klein and Morgan are still in frequent contact."

"I don't get it. Why does the good doctor have contact with a lifer like Morgan?" Clyde asked.

Bonnie stood staring out the front window above the couch. She closed the heavy drapes and abruptly sat down beside her brother.

"Uh oh, Clyde. We may have more serious problems than a dead dog. A black limo just drove by very slowly. The driver lowered his window and seemed to take a photo of our house. I couldn't see whether anyone was in the passenger seat. The windows are tinted. Two back seats might have carried passengers. I can't see a license plate number from here.

"We agreed, Bro, that revenge was our number one priority. Maybe we should have opted for witness protection, but we figured witness protection would not allow us any independence. Undercover agents would surround us for the rest of our lives. I think we should move out of here immediately, sell the cars, and disguise our appearances. I can get us a half dozen wigs and hats with ponytails hanging out at the back. And bro, you should get platform shoes or cowboy boots since you are only five foot-six."

"For now, Rosie Klein's revenge can wait and violating parole is the least of our worries. Our lives could be on the line. Fortunately, we stashed a bucket load of cash at Lober's stable where I worked on weekends. If the old tree stump is there, no way the money has been discovered," Clyde said.

"Too bad one of the horses broke your leg and caused you to have that limp, even after you healed. It could be a dead giveaway to your identity," Bonnie said.

CHAPTER SIXTEEN

Angel's Journal

After speaking with Dr. Rosie, Angel felt compelled to write her thoughts in her journal.

I know my big sister did what felt right for her. I can't hold it against her. She was loved and safe with her grandparents. I just can't help wondering what would have happened to both of us if she had stayed with me? Better still, what if her grandparents had taken me too? I could tell from Amanda that they were really nice people. They probably didn't think they had any right to me. Or they could see I would be a handful. Amanda likely told them that my bed was wet when she returned from weekends with them. I peed to try to keep Rossi from wanting to molest me. He was drunk. It didn't work. Sometimes he fell asleep in my bed and my mother would find us in the morning. She would comment on how he must have fallen asleep tucking me in. No sense telling. She wouldn't believe me, and Rossi threatened to make me pay if I told anyone. How, I wasn't quite sure? I was too scared to tell Amanda or ask if he molested her, too."

My deepest thoughts are that I could have been a wife and mother. I wanted to have sons and teach them right from wrong. They would never, ever hit a girl. I think that raising sons is far less dangerous than raising daughters. I guess it is naïve to believe that boys aren't molested too. Somehow, I think I would know if that happened. I would recognize the signs. My teachers should have recognized my neglect and abuse. Why didn't they? If I had been bad in the classroom, instead of shy and withdrawn, they would have sent me to the principal's office or guidance counselor. Maybe because they didn't get to know me. We up and moved so much.

No sense looking back. Chappy tells me that God says everything happens for a reason. We may not understand or like it. We need to gain from bad experiences and reach out to others who suffered in silence, too.

My fingers ache now from all this writing. I must admit that it makes me feel better to get it all off my chest. And it stops going round and round in my head. Maybe I have the makings of a biography.

Angel put her pencil in her journal to mark her place. She laid it under her mattress, knowing more thoughts would surface tomorrow. For now, her eyes felt heavy. She turned on her side toward the wall, pulled her blanket up over her shoulders, and prayed.

CHAPTER SEVENTEEN

Holidays With Friends and Family

Rosie and Bucky entered the Hyde Park Independent Living lobby and were immediately met by an employee wearing a smile and a badge that read, Eileen Logan, Hospitality Director.

"Good morning. Welcome to Hyde Park. How may I help you"? She asked in a pleasant voice.

"We are here to visit my parents, Esther and Caleb."

Before Rosie could complete their names Ms. Logan interrupted, "They are lovely new residents. I can show you to their apartment. Will you be staying for lunch?"

"Thank you. I am not sure what plans they may have in mind," Rosie said.

Ms. Logan pushed the button. A bell rang signifying the elevator door was opening. The three of them stepped inside. Ms. Logan pressed number three. The doors opened again, and Ms. Logan quickly stepped into the hall. Rosie noticed the security cameras in the elevator and in the hall. Spending so much time visiting county jails, it had become second nature for Rosie to observe those things.

The three of them walked down the hall, decorated with tasteful, seasonal wall hangings. At the end of the hallway, Ms. Logan tapped a bronze knocker with Esther and Caleb Cross engraved on it. Rosie noticed how high and wide the hall and wooden door were. She imagined the doorway was created to accommodate a wheelchair or additional furniture being rolled into the apartment.

Esther opened the door and stretched out her arms to hug her daughter and son-in-law. She thanked Ms. Logan for escorting them. Then Rosie's attention was drawn to the high cathedral ceiling and thought that was one of the perks of being on the top floor.

"Thank you, Eileen. We will be staying for lunch if it isn't too late to make a reservation."

"Not at all, Esther."

Rosie thought it was lovely that her mother and the director were on a first name basis. She could see Caleb seated outside on the corner screened in balcony with the view of a small park across the from the entrance. A small, tabletop Christmas tree was beside him. Her mother escorted them through the cozy living room out to where Caleb now stood. He greeted them with a smile, a firm handshake for Bucky, and a hug to his stepdaughter, Rosie.

"Welcome to our new abode. Downsizing was a pain but once it was completed, we settled in quite easily, didn't we dear? You can see the view is quite spectacular with the fountains and ducks in the pond. It is such a benefit to be in a corner unit on the top floor. Between the high ceiling and the view, we find it very serene. We watch the sun rise with our coffee and Danish. Then we have a nightcap and see the moonlight over the shimmering water in the pond."

And fancy, expensive cookware is no longer necessary. Grocery shopping at Trader Joe's usually involves wine, appetizers, and coffee. And that only occurs about once a month," Caleb said.

"We usually go to the dining room for either breakfast or lunch and then dinner if we are at home. Cocktails are always available there, but in nice weather we prefer sitting out here and enjoying our solitude," Esther added.

"The only exception to that routine is if there is a piano player singing, or a band playing or other musical entertainment. Then we make reservations with our new friends and listen or even interrupt our dining to dance," Caleb explained.

"We can see exactly why living here appeals to you both. I can see us adjusting easily to the routine you described," Rosie said.

"So, Bucky how are things going at the university? Still enjoying your job?" Caleb asked.

"I do enjoy it. We both like watching sports and Toledo has great football and basketball teams. Of course, my passion, baseball is played in the Spring. We love watching the young men and women develop in sports, graduate, and move on to careers," Bucky replied.

After a light lunch of grilled chicken on a bed of lettuce with craisins, walnuts, and goat cheese, Rosie excused herself to call Stella.

"Hi Stella. We are here at Mom's retirement center. It is lovely. Have you heard of Hyde Park Independent Living?"

"Yes, our choir sang there earlier this month. It followed a luncheon."

"We just had lunch here. Food and service are excellent."

"So, when can we expect you guys?" Stella asked.

"How about five o'clock? We will hang out here and make plans to be with them and open gifts tomorrow. Then we will head over. Is there anything I can bring?"

"Absolutely not. Just plan to relax and leave your worries behind. Sorry about leaving your cat. Did you say her name is Willow?"

"Yes. She thinks she is a dog in many ways. Can you believe she comes when she is called? I have a lot to tell you, Roomie. See you soon. And we will bring the wine."

As Rosie and Bucky enjoyed a glass of wine, poured carefully by Stella, Travis asked. "Rosie, tell us more about your interest in that inmate, Angel Morgan, is it? Devon needs to hear this story too."

Devon, his wife, Brenda, Stella, and Travis were seated on an oval, sectional, white leather couch across from Rosie and Bucky who were sitting on two tall matching plaid armchairs with a small glass top table between them.

"I think I have discussed her case with you back when you both helped me evaluate another defendant, Randy Evans. Angel is serving life without parole. She has been at the Ohio Reformatory for Women for the past twenty-five years or so. She was part of a little gang in Toledo and agreed to a plea deal in exchange for testifying against the two male shooters she was allegedly with. She has been on my mind through the years because I didn't think she could understand what she was signing."

"What made you think that? Was it a low I.Q. or mental illness?"

"Her measured I.Q. at the time was low, but probably impacted by her lack of education, environmental deprivation, and stressful circumstances." Rosie responded.

"Was she represented by a public defender from Lucas County?" Devon asked, peering over his horn-rimmed glasses. "I went to law school with a few guys who ended up working there."

"No. Her attorney was a prominent local defense attorney appointed by the Judge for her case."

"I see," Travis said. After years of practicing law, he saw the writing on the wall. A private attorney loses money when appointed to represent an indigent client.

Rosie remembered how proud Travis was of his son, Devon's, sharp mind, and inquisitive nature when he was just a young teen. It appeared to Rosie that Devon's question regarding Angel's representation was evidence of just that. It suited a career in law beautifully, she thought. She knew from experience that Travis was a very thorough attorney, and according to Stella, a very deep thinker. So as far as their son, Devon went, the apple didn't fall far from the tree.

Rosie continued. "At the time, it was presumed that Angel was a part of each of six murders. Several were random and others carefully planned and executed. Literally speaking, they executed two of their friends because they were afraid, they would narc. When I visited her in prison recently, it came to my attention that she wasn't even with them during the first murder."

"You mean, not in the car? I think I remember that it was at a phone booth, right?" Travis asked.

"Yes. I told her the entire case was reenacted on Oxygen television, commemorating the twenty-five-year anniversary of the crime spree."

"Did it surprise her? She had to be terribly distressed by the newspaper's reminder," Devon said.

"I think it did surprise her. She appeared very upset to hear Toledo was still remembering their crime spree after all these years. I felt sorry that I informed her of that article," Rosie said.

Rosie decided that Devon was not only a talented attorney, but also a compassionate man. Rosie said, "what she said next was a total surprise to me. I thought the passenger in the front seat shot the kid at the phone booth. Angel and three others were riding in the back seat. The TV program showed three kids wearing dark hoodies walking on the sidewalk toward the phone booth."

"What was did she say, Rosie?" Stella, who was listening to the story, asked.

"She told me that they might have been walking. She wasn't with them."

"Did she say she was charged with murder for that crime?"

"Yes, she thought they did. Some memories are blurred. She didn't remember me evaluating her and I saw her on six separate occasions. The detectives assumed she was with them since their joy ride was seen by several witnesses who were on foot nearby. Of course, the witnesses couldn't identify the suspects. It was early evening, but dark. They were able to describe the car, and two males and a female, that they saw leaving the scene. They ran over to render aid to the young man sprawled on the sidewalk, but he was lying in a pool of blood, and they presumed he was dead. They called 911 and waited until the cops and ambulance arrived. Their judgment proved to be correct. The EMTs pronounced him dead and zipped him into a black body bag."

"Based on that piece of information, it seems that Angel was indicted on at least one murder charge that failed to place her at the scene at all, "Devon said.

"There's likely a lot more to the story, but let's end the conversation for now and enjoy our evening, okay?"

"I agree, Travis," Stella said."

"Nothing is going to happen overnight, that's for sure," Travis said. "I do have some ideas to share with you, Rosie. If you want to intervene for her, I know who might need to be apprised of your information."

They all adjourned to the dining room and tabled further discussion until later.

"So, have you considered contacting the Ohio Governor on Angel's behalf?" Travis asked as they sat enjoying their coffee with Irish Cream in front of the fireplace.

"I have had fleeting thoughts about doing something like that. Yes, that has crossed my mind. It's just that who she was when all the crimes occurred, and who she is today, are two different things. Punishing her no longer has to do with protecting the community. I don't for one second see her as a threat. She has been truly rehabilitated. One of very few inmates who are remorseful and will not repeat their shameful behavior ever again." Rosie's voice quaked. Bucky squeezed her arm. She took a deep breath and continued.

"I believe that her faith in God is genuine, and she will follow the path she believes God has prepared for her. But the media and the Toledo community were so appalled by the serious nature of the crimes, that they don't want her or anyone in her little group to see the world outside those steel bars. I feel compassion for the victims' families."

"Consider it, Rosie," Travis said. "If your description of this woman is accurate, she has references who would speak in her behalf. Other than you, it sounds like she has a Chaplain, a case manager, and a medic who could provide information to a parole board or to a government official, such as the Governor, regarding her character. You also mentioned how she has helped other inmates and is dedicated to her work in the sewing workshop."

"All of that is true, Travis. I may send our Senators or the Governor a letter. At the very least, it could result in her receiving more privileges, such as being permitted to take community college classes on-line. She would be extremely grateful to be able to do that. She wants to improve herself and learn more about how to help others to help themselves. She also spoke of being the chaplain's assistant if she competes a certification program."

"I know you've had a long day, Rosie. Why don't I show you and Bucky to your room and give you the towels and things you might need to be comfortable?" Stella interrupted and redirected the conversation.

"We can talk more tomorrow. Devon and I will take a little road trip to Marysville to visit Angel. I will need the details as to how I get approved. If she designates me as her lawyer, then it is a slam-dunk. When you talk to her next, you might want to tell her we are willing to meet with her."

Rosie sighed a sigh of relief. "That would be great, Travis," she said as she and Bucky stood to follow Stella to their room.

CHAPTER EIGHTEEN

Angel's Grandma

It was a cold Sunday morning. Angel watched Rock City. She loved that weekly Christian church broadcast. She sang along with the hymns, got a lot from the pastor's message about love and redemption, and praised Jesus for her blessings. She tried hard to be grateful even if she was simply grateful to be breathing one more day.

Usually, it lifted her lonely spirit. It took her mind off herself. She would pray silently for other people who she knew needed prayer. But today, Angel had a distressing conversation with her grandmother. She abruptly hung up the phone before her allotted time was up. She shook her head and slowly walked back to her room, acknowledging no one who was passing by. She sat on the side of her bed, rocking back and forth, as she had begun doing in childhood to soothe herself when she was distressed. Tears streamed down her cheeks. She didn't wipe them off. They dampened her uniform.

All Angel could think about was how much of a loser she is. She wished she could talk to Dr. Rosie, but she was so ashamed she doubted she could really tell her how she felt. She picked up her journal from beneath the mattress. She leaned back against the wall with her knees up so she could prop the journal up to write.

First of all, she wrote, *how could my mother have had another kid? She must have been pregnant when she went to prison. Then what? Grandma is sort of vague about it all. I think she hides things from me to not hurt me or worry me or something.*

Grandma had told her that her twenty-five-year younger sister almost died from an overdose of Heroin laced with Fentanyl. She was expected to survive. To make matters worse, there were scars on her arms that weren't from shooting up. Apparently, she had been cutting herself.

"If I was out there, maybe I could save her from the road she's been on and will continue to travel."

Angel remembered Grandma saying, "Angel if you had not been sent to prison, you would likely have been dead or too messed up to help yourself, let alone anyone else."

But that didn't make Angel feel better or less guilty. Grandma just didn't get it, she thought. She asked Grandma, "what's my little sister's name and why haven't you mentioned her before now?"

Grandma hesitated and then softly said, "Amy." She tried to explain. "Angel, I didn't want to worry you when there is nothing, you can do about this."

"I will pray for Amy. That is the least I can do." Angel wrote through her tears. *"When Chappy gets back, I will ask Chappy to pray, and I will let Dr. Rosie know what I am dealing with, too."*

Angel, too harsh with her old grandmother who would be ninety in three years, remembered a quote *"Christmas is not the time to hurt someone you love just because they unintentionally hurt you."*

CHAPTER NINETEEN

Christmas With Family

"Bucky, I am thrilled that both boys and most of their families can join us for Christmas Eve dinner. I can't believe they both moved back to Ohio to continue careers near us."

"I know how much it means to you, Rosie."

"I' m sorry that your girls live way up in Alaska. At least they live close to each other. How cool that both their husbands ended up at the same military base for the time being, right?"

Bucky nodded in agreement and said, "Thank goodness for facetime. It helps a lot."

"Well, we've been married so long that my sons and families consider you part of their families, too. As for this visit, I think Christopher, Lynn, Josh and his cute little wife, Janie, should stay in the two bedrooms upstairs. Isn't it great that Janie is pregnant with our first great-grandchild?"

"Makes me feel ancient. Just kidding, Precious." They both laughed.

"Too bad both our granddaughters, Dottie and Beth, can't be here. When Christopher called last week, he told me that Beth has been deployed to Iraq again. Her medical career with the Air Force keeps involving dangerous, war-torn areas.

And then Stephen called and told me that Dottie is in France for the upcoming semester studying musical theater. She just took the opportunity to audition for a part in Cabaret that will be opening soon at the Lido 2 in Paris. She got a part with a few speaking lines, in English, numerous dance routines, and a vocal solo. The show will be opening in late January and so she couldn't miss rehearsals to come home. He said she has a voice teacher who is not just teaching her to sing, but also to beef up her French language skills."

"That's quite an opportunity, don't you think?" Bucky asked.

"Yes. By the way, I think Stephen, Louise, and Oliver will be comfortable in the garage loft. Does that sound good to you? Maybe they will stay longer, since all three are on winter break from their school responsibilities. It's neat that Stephen and Louise are professors at Oberlin in the same department and Oliver's doctoral graduate assistantship enables him to teach on-line."

"Yes, dear. As you said, it is definitely neat," Bucky chuckled a little to himself.

"That's fine. You aren't putting Stephen's family in the loft because they have two dogs, are you?" Now Bucky laughed out loud.

"Of course, not silly. The dogs are welcome in the house. To tell you the truth, I think Willow will rule. She has no fear. She will whip those big dogs into shape in no time at all."

***

"Bucky, can you please get the door? I am setting out the fondue pot filled with peanut oil."

"Sure, Precious," Bucky said as he put down his intriguing Grisham novel and reading glasses.

"Welcome," Bucky opened the door. There stood Louise grinning from ear to ear, with bags of wrapped gifts. Bucky took them from her outstretched arms, set them on the bench, and gave her a big bear hug. Christmas Eve was very traditional with the same meal each year, stemming from their childhood. Stephen and Oliver stepped into the foyer behind Louise. Oliver held both golden retrievers by their leashes. They were obediently standing still on each side of him.

Rosie approached the group and was greeted with hugs and kisses. They removed their coats and boots and moved with the animals into the family room where a blazing fire was waiting to warm their chilly hands and feet and the nativity scene was displayed on the mantel. Rosie asked the names of the dogs and bent to pet them.

"This is Rocky, and this is Moose," Oliver said. "You wouldn't believe how small and scrawny they were when we adopted them from the shelter."

Louise noticed Willow, perched on top of the baby grand in the midst of family photos. She approached the piano. Willow did not budge, allowing Louise to pet her but skeptically eyeing both dogs whose tails were wagging, and noses were pointed toward her.

They no sooner gave Bucky their drink orders than the doorbell rang again. This time Rosie went to the door. Christopher, Lynn, Josh, and a very pregnant Janie, stood there with broad smiles.

"Welcome. Goodness, Josh, and Janie. I haven't seen you since your wedding at The Rock of Gibraltar. What a beautiful event that was." Rosie kissed her grandson and granddaughter-in-law. Christopher and Lynn gave her a group hug. All outer garments removed; the group joined the rest of the family in the family room.

For dinner, Rosie served light appetizers of shrimp, olives stuffed with feta cheese, rye crackers, Boursin Fig and Balsamic cheese spread, and lobster wrapped in bacon. Drinks offered were non-alcoholic sparkling wine, hot or chilled spiced eggnog, and Shiraz red wine. Conversation focused on the new log home, the two very obedient dogs, Willow, the absent granddaughters, and the forthcoming baby. She wondered if they know what gender they're having, and do they have names selected? She decided it was a delicate subject and not to be brought up by her.

Dinner was served around a large, oak, circular table that comfortably sat nine. It was set with Rosie's mother's dishes, on a colorful holiday tablecloth. New England Clam Chowder was the first course. Caesar Salad, scalloped potatoes, and their meat selections completed the main course. Steak or chicken were the options for quick, deep frying in a pot of sizzling oil. Warm Terriyaki sauce or the sauce created by the potatoes, along with hot rolls and butter completed the meal. Rosie noticed that Janie limited her carbs and Josh, on the other hand, ate his little wife's share of potatoes, rolls, and red meat.

After dinner, Rosie suggested that everyone settle into their respective rooms and return for a light dessert, featuring peppermint ice cream, and a hot toddy. Christopher and Josh put on their boots and ran quickly out to their jeep in the driveway to retrieve their suitcases and a basket of gifts. Bucky hopped into the passenger seat of Stephen's Honda Odyssey, and he, Stephen, and Oliver, headed to the garage loft to deposit their belongings and turn up the heat. When they returned, they brought the dogs' water bowls but left the dog food back in the loft for the time being. Bucky glanced around the property just in case they had uninvited visitors.

Conversation began with Louise announcing that they are going over to France for Dottie's opening night and the matinee on the following day. She said, "the Lido 2, unlike the original Lido has theatre seating. No dinner is served. It holds one thousand patrons, and we have front row seating."

"Where is Dottie staying and for how long?" Rosie asked.

"She is in a youth hostel in what is known as the sixth district. She has five roommates and they each have a free-standing closet that they lock their belongings in when they're gone. It is across from the Luxembourg Palace. To get to school or to the theatre they walk through a gate and cut through the palace gardens to the metro station. They are in school until noon. She and two other girls catch a quick lunch at an outdoor café and head to the theatre for rehearsal. If this opportunity had not arisen, she would have returned for the second semester. Now, we wonder if she'll take a year or more off, depending on how long the show remains," Stephen explained.

"Christopher, what about Beth? Second lieutenant right out of college, right?"

"Yup, she was recruited by the Air Force right after her sophomore year. They saw her potential for leadership. We didn't mention it to you because enlistment wasn't finalized until graduation. Little did Beth know, as an officer, she'd be deployed twice to the middle East."

"We have prayer warriors at church. We will pray for her safety and health," Rosie said.

"Thanks, Mom. She is not on the front lines. But a mysterious ailment seems to be rearing its ugly head, particularly in the officers' quarters. Someone from the States must have contracted it and spread it. It is called Covid 19. Symptoms include severe coughing spells, headache, low grade fever, and get this, loss of sense of taste and smell. Weird," Christopher said.

"Hopefully being young and fit will mean they won't get seriously ill. Strange though, Beth said one of her roommates threw out an unopened jar of dill pickles because she thought it was rancid. It turned out that it was her and not the pickles," Louise said.

"Uh, oh. Not a good sign. That's an unusual symptom," Stephen said.

After dessert they all bundled up and drove in two cars to the candlelight service at Oak Creek Christian Church. The snowplows had come through and Rosie thought how grateful she was that Lucas County took care of the roads immediately after a heavy snow fall.

Looking out the window, Rosie's thoughts turned to her pen pal, Angel, Rosie couldn't help but wonder how Angel was really doing on this special night of the holiday season. Rosie didn't realize that while celebrating with her family, she had missed a tearful call from Angel who desperately needed to hear Rosie's voice on a dark, lonely Christmas Eve.

CHAPTER TWENTY

Angel's Call

Rosie leaned back in the wingback chair in her Summerhill office, propped her legs up on the ottoman and prepared to receive Angel's pre-arranged call. Willow immediately hopped up into her lap. She had told Ruth she was expecting the call and to run interference if anyone was wanting to talk to her. The call came in on time and Rosie accepted the charges.

"Happy New Year Dr. Rosie," Angel said.

"Happy New Year, Angel," Rosie responded. "How are you this afternoon. Have you worked this week?"

"No, because of the holidays, we don't begin sewing again until tomorrow. These are United States flags. You know we sew all kinds of flags. We have even sewed sports team flags and State flags."

"I hadn't given much thought to what kind of flag you sew. Interesting."

"I'm about to watch my very favorite pro player, Tom Brady. I love football season. It gives me something to look forward to each week and lets off some of my steam, in an appropriate way, no cussing, of course." Heather laughed.

"How fun. Do you watch just the Patriots or other pro and college teams?" Rosie asked.

"Any kind of football, but mostly I follow Brady. If he changes teams, and they say he will, then I will cheer for that team. How about you, Dr. Rosie? Do you have a favorite player or team?"

"Bucky loves football. His job as athletic director for the University of Toledo provides us with lots of opportunities to go to games, even high school. Part of his job is recruiting players. As far as professional football teams go, we tend to be Cincinnati Bengals fans. And for baseball, we love the Cincinnati Reds. Did you know he was the head baseball coach at Toledo before being promoted to athletic director? And now he is back there as interim Athletic Director."

"I think I remember you telling me that. It was before you came back into my life, right?"

"Yes. Baseball was his first passion. He played college ball, himself. Recently, he was inducted into the Toledo Softball Hall of Fame for his post-college softball hobby. Ha. It was almost like a career. I didn't know him. I guess he played several nights a week and at week-end tournaments."

"And you were some kind of dancer for basketball, Dr. Rosie?"

"I was what we called a dancing Rockette. The name comes from the fact that the University of Toledo teams are called the Rockets. There were twenty-four of us and we entertained the fans at half-time of all the home basketball games. We danced to songs from musical films from the 50's and 60's. Obviously they were popular long before your time, Angel."

"That is so cool. I wonder what hobbies or talents I would have had if I had grown up in a different family. My grandmother said I wanted to take ballet and would run around the house on my tip toes. Of course, my mother never permitted that. She wouldn't pay for it, and she saw no use to it."

Rosie could hear Angel's heavy breathing. She thought she would try to calm her thoughts. "So, dancing in prison has been sort of a blessing, hasn't it?" Rosie asked.

"Absolutely. Can you believe we have dance classes other than praise dancing? The teacher is a volunteer from a local dance studio. She stands on the stage where your visitation occurred. We face her and she turns on recorded country music and teaches us line dancing. I love it. I practice alone in between classes."

"I didn't know that. How nice."

"When we face long stretches of quarantine for punishment, disciplinary measures they call it, or illness, dancing alone keeps me from going nuts. I stand next to my bed and dance. I have songs recorded or I have the tunes and words in my head."

"Wow. That's sad in some ways, of course, but amazing that you can pull up the melodies and words from your head. That is real talent. Angel, I have something important to talk to you about, Angel. I have a lawyer friend who has taken an interest in you. He would like to visit you as a professional, not a casual friend."

"Oh, my gosh. That is such great news, Dr. Rosie. I can make him my new representative. A representative isn't necessarily a lawyer. It can be anyone who takes an interest in an inmate's well-being. Some reps are Priests, or Pastors, and some are social services folks. No one outside of prison employees has ever taken an interest in me or my case," Angel replied cheerfully.

"His name is Attorney Travis Gump. His son, Devon Gump, is also an attorney in his firm. They practice in the Dayton area. They will drive up to Marysville and talk privately to you."

"I will fill out a form with my case manager, Mrs. Marigold, and that will identify them and allow me to see them in the professional area instead of the common visitation area where we met."

"I can contact Mrs. Marigold, too, Angel. And I will let the attorneys know you have agreed to be represented by them."

"I don't have any money, Dr. Rosie." Angel's voice lowered. Her concern was obvious.

"Trust me. You won't owe them anything. They are genuinely kind and longtime friends of mine."

"I have prayed for a miracle and having them lawyers to talk to qualifies. Even if nothing changes for me, I appreciate what you have done for me, Dr. Rosie. And your friendship means the world to me."

"Thank you, Angel. Getting to take on-line college classes might just come of the lawyer's intervention. So, stay positive and email me when the Gump's are approved to visit. Meanwhile, enjoy that football game."

"I will, Dr. Rosie. What a year this will be."

***

As much as Angel loves football and particularly any game featuring Tom Brady, after her conversation with Dr. Rosie, she found it difficult to keep her attention on this game. Her mood was elevated regardless of the score and for the first time, her thoughts turned to what life might be on the outside of these bars and prison walls.

Even if these lawyers and Dr. Rosie could begin a process leading to a parole hearing, Angel knew it would take a long time. She wondered if meanwhile she would be allowed to take on-line classes through an Ohio based Community College, if a parole hearing was in the works. Ordinarily she doubted it would be permitted. But with the lawyers working on her case, and fervent prayer on the part of Chappy, Dr. Rosie, and herself, it could result in approval.

Then she began to think about what skills, other than sewing, she could develop in those classes that would help her get a job and in what community? Being a convicted felon would limit her opportunities. She figured she would not be able to work with children or older adults and probably not in a job handling money. What employer would trust her not to rob or endanger others and not be tempted to steal from a company?

Then her mind turned to where she could live with no money for an apartment and no family to take her in. What kind of temporary shelter or housing would be available? Last time she was in that situation she made terrible, rash decisions that resulted in living a life behind bars.

CHAPTER TWENTY-ONE

Get the Ball Rolling

"Good morning, Angel. What's going on? You wanted to speak with me?" Mrs. Marigold asked.

"Yes, Ma'am, I need to fill out some paperwork so that two representatives can begin professional visits with me." Angel said cheerfully.

"That is good news." Mrs. Marigold stood up from behind her desk and picked up a folder from her four-drawer file cabinet. She sat back down and handed two forms, one for each representative, to Angel. "You can fill these out here if you know the information required. Or you can call someone who does know. Might I ask what profession these representatives are?"

"Yes. They are lawyers that Dr. Rosie knows. She said she will be calling you. They need to be approved so that we can meet in a private interview room. In some ways it would be a good idea for Dr. Rosie's visit to be considered professional, but then we wouldn't have access to food and snacks, would we?"

"That's true. You wouldn't be able to order food or have any more pictures taken. It's your decision, Angel."

"I will take the forms with me. Dr. Rosie will e-mail me the information required. She has their addresses and other personal information. Then I should have them back to you by tomorrow."

"That sounds perfect. I can fax them to the warden who needs to approve their applications. I think they can schedule visits beginning the first of next week. They are not limited to the visiting hours of family and friends. They are welcome to see you at any time of day."

"That's cool. I will have a lot of questions to ask you, Mrs. Marigold, once I have met with them. They are father and son lawyers. Isn't that cool? I think being a lawyer would be neat. Then again, being a case manager or a psychologist would be a way to help others. I truly want to help other women, so they don't end up here, like me."

"I know you have a compassionate heart, Angel. We all recognize the nice things you do to help the new inmates adjust and to provide them with necessities."

"I can't believe when they arrive here from county jails, they come without anything. No hygiene products, other than a toothbrush and small tube of toothpaste. So usually, when I buy stuff from the catalog, I order two of the basic things so I can share with them. I am not the only one who does that, Mrs. Marigold. Believe it or not, lifers care about other women. Because we know what it is like to feel unloved, afraid, and helpless. New socks, underwear, sanitary napkins, shampoo, a hairbrush, and even a package of instant soup or noodles, goes to show them they are not forgotten and alone."

"You are so right. Have a nice day, Angel."

Angel quickly returned to her bedside to check to see whether she had received an e-mail from Dr. Rosie. She didn't want to waste any time filling out the forms. She trusted Dr. Rosie yet felt nervous that the two attorneys would change their minds. If they read the twenty-fifth anniversary article about their crime spree, they might not think she was worth the effort. Or they would figure it is useless to try to convince authorities to hear what they have to say on her behalf.

Angel knelt down beside her bed and prayed for God's forgiveness and grace.

CHAPTER TWENTY-TWO

Investigations Continue

"Happy New Year to you both," Ron said as he joined Wes and Rosie in the same booth in the Embassy Restaurant Pub that they had graced two weeks prior.

"It should be an exceptional year, in my opinion," Wes responded.

"I agree. For starters, there are no major storms forecast this winter. My husband and I bought a log home on ten acres about ten miles South of town. I enjoy looking at the snow, but I am not a fan of driving country roads with it diminishing my vision."

"I agree, Rosie," Ron said.

"Here's what I have been doing," Wes said. "I spoke to some people who knew Angel's history, firsthand. They worked at the Juvenile Court. One woman worked in the kitchen and a couple others were counselors way back when she was there for grand theft auto. They said it was obvious to them that she never stole the vehicle that she was found red handed with. She was homeless and was asleep in it. She didn't even have the keys. They don't know if she was covering for someone who stole it, or it had been abandoned. It was parked behind a church where she probably felt safe."

"So, it seems like she has been a victim of circumstances all of her life, doesn't it Rosie?" Ron asked.

"She will describe herself as having been a loser and says she wasn't a nice girl back then. She blames herself for making poor choices," Rosie said.

"There's more. I was told that a maintenance guy was fired while Angel was there. Another girl told a counselor that he approached her inappropriately in a hallway and Angel told her to get to her room. The girl thinks that Angel protected her and likely was abused by him instead of her. As far as the counselor knew, Angel never reported him or told anyone."

"That's unbelievable that she would protect a younger girl, knowing what was likely in store for her."

"Right. It certainly speaks to her character, doesn't it?"

"She hasn't stopped helping others. Well, I guess she did for the first five years in Marysville. She told me she was very angry and lashed out by fighting, shoving, and cursing. This resulted in what she called "time in the hole," cold, scared, and alone."

"That is terrible."

"From what I can tell, this means solitary confinement without light or contact from anyone on the outside. She described it as having one, dangling ceiling lightbulb, a metal bench, an open toilet, and a slot in the door for a food tray twice a day. In the morning, she received two glazed donuts and a cup of look warm, weak, black coffee."

"Geez. Do you mean that for five years she repeatedly ended up in solitary confinement? You'd think she'd learn self-control to avoid such harsh punishment."

"You would think that. But other inmates provoked her knowing she had a short fuse. It was entertaining to them when she lashed out at someone else. The inmates blamed her if anything came up missing. Of course, the officers believed them. One time, an officer's cell phone got misplaced and she was put into solitary for stealing it. Later, while she was still in solitary, it turned up. Then they knew she couldn't have taken it and was set up by another inmate.

She finally came to the attention of the Chaplain Bennett. Chaplain Bennett began visiting her and showing her compassion. Angel began setting an example for the new inmates so they wouldn't experience the same emotions she had displayed."

"Thank heavens for the Chaplain and whoever brought Angel to her attention."

"Angel didn't tell me all of this. But I think the next Chaplain that she calls Chappy, might have grown up in less-than-ideal family circumstances. I plan to talk to her this coming week. I don't think she was ever a delinquent but possibly endured neglect and abuse."

CHAPTER TWENTY-THREE

Angel's Evening Journal Entry

I'm so happy that Dr. Rosie's coming back for my birthday. I don't expect any gifts. She has done so much already. And Mrs. Marigold gave me the gym shoes and socks that Dr. Rosie brought her to give to me. My feet are much more comfortable now. No new blisters. And for Christmas Dr. Rosie ordered the beautiful silver cross necklace and leather-bound journals that I wanted. She thought I was giving one away. I explained how I use both journals each day. One I write in as soon as I get up in the morning. I told her that I do give snacks and sodas to women who have nothing in their commissary account but that I write in one journal first thing in the morning and one in bed at night. In the morning, I write my blessings and prayers for myself and others. In the evening, I write my feelings and thoughts about how the day went. Some nights all I can think of is that I am grateful the day is over.

CHAPTER TWENTY-FOUR

The Sheriff's Call

"Telephone for you, Rosie. It's the sheriff. I answered your phone because you stepped outside to fill the bird feeders."

"Thanks, Bucky. Good evening, Sheriff," Rosie said.

"Did I hear Bucky say you were out in the snow feeding the birds?"

"Yup. We have two bird houses and two bird feeders. We don't want them to starve in the winter." Rosie laughed as she took off her wool cap, and gloves. Bucky placed a cup of steaming, hot chocolate with whipped cream on the side table where Rosie seated herself.

"You probably wonder why I'm calling after hours. It's about Bonnie and Clyde. Thought you'd want to know that they violated parole and have escaped the country. They dressed as airline attendants. Being employees allowed them to fly standby, free, without showing identification or boarding passes. The last we know of them; they landed in St. Martin. Then they vanished."

"St. Martin? Bucky and I honeymooned there at the Saphire Beach Club and recently returned to celebrate our twenty-fifth anniversary. It is such a lovely Island. The turquoise water is so clear. The Dutch side has a port where the cruise ships dock each week. The tourists can visit a casino, shop and eat. There are lots of jewelry stores and outdoor booths with handmade purses and jewelry made by local residents. The French side has beautiful soft, sand beaches and restaurants featuring French cuisine. Could they have managed to board a cruise ship?"

"That's a good thought but I doubt it. The ships, as you know, are enormous and seem to have tight security when passengers reboard. We saw them on the security video at the St. Martin airport when they arrived."

"Another thought is this. Bucky and I took a catamaran to St. Kitts Island one day and a high-speed ferry to St. Barts another day. It would be easy for them to rent a little villa with American dollars on any of those Islands. No questions asked."

"The good news, Rosie, is that you appear to be safe. And I am very sorry about the loss of your dog."

"Thank you."

CHAPTER TWENTY-FIVE

St. Martin Hide-Away

"Clyde, the smoke burns my eyes, makes them water, and makes my wigs smell. I don't think grilling ribs on the beach is going to work for me." Bonnie said as she wiped the streaks of mascara from her cheeks.

"What if I grill, Bonnie, and you put the grilled veggies and ribs on the customer's plates, along with a tall, narrow, shot glass filled with Tequilla and topped with a slice of lime? Oh, and don't forget the Montgomery Inn Barbecue Sauce." Clyde laughed. Bonnie put her hands on her hips and said, "Okay, I'll give it a try. If I serve them their food, they're more likely to leave a tip. If they pick up the orders at the shack, they won't tip. Of course, Europeans never tip anyhow."

"Be your sweet self, Bonnie. Smile and tell them to have a seat under an umbrella. As you can see, the tables with umbrellas fill up quickly because they protect customers from the sun and the birds."

"True. And they're less likely to steal the barbecue sauce with me standing nearby. I think we got really lucky that Big Uncle John is driving a cab and has a small studio apartment behind his house. To be sure we have the rent money he is charging, he will definitely direct tourists to this beach and emphasize how good our ribs are."

"You are right, Bonnie. He really is big, isn't he? You figure he goes four hundred pounds? Mom used to nag her brother, John, about losing weight. Young Cindy did too. Lucky, we kept our mouths shut. Uncle John seems to really like us."

"I would think four hundred is close," Bonnie laughed." I don't imagine he visits the nude beach that he takes his tourists to on his day off."

"At least he has never offered me a ride there," Clyde said. They both laughed.

Bonnie relaxed in a chaise lounge with a cigarette and a shot of Tequila. "Hey, bro, I'm beginning to think we might be safe here. The authorities would assume we skipped to Canada since Michigan is on the border and we used to traffic those kids to Windsor."

Clyde stood behind his sister, took a deep drag, and gazed at the outgoing tide. He patted her on top of her frizzy wig and said, "You're probably right, Bonnie. You always have been."

CHAPTER TWENTY-SIX

Rosie's Second Visit

Angel was accompanied to the professional conference room by Officer Verna Mitchell, who just transferred from the Lucas County Detention Center to live close to her daughter. Retirement is next year and then she will have the opportunity to babysit her three grandchildren while her daughter works as a cook at the popular, quaint, Amish Grill.

"Do you remember me, Officer Mitchell? You were so kind to me when I was waiting trial in that Lucas County Jail."

"Of course I do, Angel. You were always appreciative that I brought you snacks and escorted you without handcuffs," Officer Mitchell said with kindness in her voice. She opened the door for Angel to join Dr. Rosie who was already seated at the table.

"Good morning, Angel. Happy early birthday."

"Thank you, Dr. Rosie," Angel said. Officer Mitchell smiled. She nodded at Rosie as she left the room slowly and locked the door.

"Angel, I need to ask you something. Wes Hall, an investigative reporter from the Toledo Blade interviewed a counselor who knew you at the juvenile detention center. Do you remember Jennifer Keane? She thinks you were sexually assaulted by a maintenance man during your time there. Were you?"

Rosie leaned forward and looked directly at Angel. Angel sat back in her chair, paused, sighed, and looked up at the ceiling. She leaned forward, clasped her hands together on the table, and with her head down, answered, "Yes, more than one time."

"I'm so very sorry," Rosie said as she shook her head in dismay. He was fired but no charges were ever brought against him. Did you tell anyone?"

"No. He threatened me saying if I told, he would deny it, and everyone knew I was nothing but a liar. He also put a broomstick to my throat and said he could really hurt me." Angel's voice wavered.

"Did anyone ever interview you about it?"

Angel nodded yes but did not lift her head. "I guess a younger girl that shared a bunk with me told that I protected her from him. Sot the counselor, that Jennifer Keane, talked to me but I denied it."

"Did anyone else know?"

" There probably could have been other victims. Girls talk. There was no conversation about him other than that he was mean and dirty. In some ways I was like a big sister to them."

"Because of your age?"

"Sort of. But more likely because I knew how the system worked. And I am ashamed to say, my size. I weighed over two hundred and I'm short, you know. They weighed me when I was arrested. The medic did blood work to see if I had used drugs or alcohol."

"You know that we are now permitted to meet here in this area because this is considered a professional visit. I am helping your lawyers. You are allowed to hand me notes and other written materials. I know a lot about your background. If your memories surface that no one has been told about, it is important for you to write them down for me. Can you do that? Is it okay?"

"Sure. When you bring something up, it sort of jars my memory."

"Do you remember sleeping in the stolen car behind the church? Was anyone with you? How did you get there?"

"Well, obviously when I was arrested, no one was with me. I was high and sitting on a park bench across the street from the church. I don't know why I always did that. I would walk around until I found somewhere to sit near a church. It might go back to that church that I loved when I was a little girl."

"Probably so, Angel."

" It was so dark and cold. No moon at all that night. The car drove slowly by. I watched it being driven into the parking lot behind the church. Then a police cruiser drove by. I think it spooked the kids in the car and they shut off the motor and ran off into a wood area. I waited. My toes and fingers felt numb. The cops didn't return. So, I went over and got in the car, fell asleep or passed out. Next thing I know, I was

hauled out of it by my coat collar and shoved into a cop car."
"Did they ask you how you came to be sleeping in the car or for your
identification?"

"I think I gave them a smart aleck answer and told them my ID was
stolen."

"What happened next?"

"They searched the car and trunk for drugs or bodies, maybe."

"Did they find anything?"

"No, surprisingly. Not even keys or money. If I stole the car, I
would have had the keys."

"Then what did they say?"

"They asked where I lived and if I was with the driver, or knew the
owner? I said I'm on my way to my grandparents' house in Florida. It
wasn't true but I was scared and didn't know what to say. My
grandparents were a lot younger then and, in the winter, they lived at
The Villages about an hour from Orlando. The sad thing is, I never saw
my grandpa alive again. He died the next year from a stroke. Grandma
sold the house in Florida and has stayed year-round in Ohio. She says it
makes her feel closer to me even though she never comes here to see
me."

"Did they read you your rights?"

"Yes, I was charged with grand theft auto. Honest, Dr. Rosie, I
never drove that car or knew those kids. I didn't have a license because I
entered juvenile the first time before I was old enough to drive." Angel
hung her head and shook it from side to side.

"So, you are saying that as far as you knew, you were the only one
held accountable for the theft of that vehicle."

"Yes, they never looked for anyone else," Angel said as she looked
directly at Dr. Rosie and sounding more animated.

Rosie took notes to remind herself of contacts she wanted to make,
if possible, regarding Angel's juvenile detention sentence. While arrest
reports might not be disclosable for juvenile offenders, records of dates
of employment of arresting officers, staff and correction officers would
possibly be obtainable. She thought Wes would know how to go about
getting that information. He was well known for his investigative
techniques and knowledge.

Rosie handed Angel some unlined paper and asked her to draw a picture of her pain. It could be physical or emotional. She handed her a set of colored pencils. Angel looked clueless. Rosie explained, "Just draw whatever comes to mind when you think of or experience severe pain."

Angel drew large red circles that filled the paper. Then Angel said, "draw what your pain getting better would look like, Angel."

Angel used pink pencils of two different shades to draw small circles that filled the paper.

Lastly, Rosie said, "Please draw a picture of what life would look like without pain."

Angel asked, "Should I put myself in the picture?" Rosie nodded yes. Angel drew a green tree with red blossoms of different sizes blooming. She drew herself, in rolled up jeans and barefooted, sitting on the grass, leaning against the tree, reading a book to a group of little children.

Rosie said, "That's a great job. I want you to draw in your journal along with writing, Angel. It is called a right brain activity. It doesn't take your pain away, but it distracts you from feeling it so intently and provides hope."

"Cool. I understand. I will do that."

"Have you thought about what you would do for a living and where you would live when you get out?"

"I used to want to cut and style hair. It has been so many years, and with my aches and pains, I think at this point I'd like to help abused women in a shelter."

"It sounds like a fine, realistic plan."

"What's the use of thinking about it. I'll never get out on parole."

"Judge Brown might not be influenced by public opinion at this time of her career, Angel. She showed compassion when she sentenced you for all your crimes to be served concurrently. Your testimony and genuine display of remorse moved her. She might expect you to start a fresh life in a different community."

"Yes, I've been thinking. If I ever am allowed to leave the State, my brothers said I could work in their ice cream and coffee shop. Then I might even take some night classes at an adult education center. I could afford to live in a small apartment of my own not far from work or school."

"That's a great idea," Rosie responded enthusiastically. Then she slid a birthday card across the table to Angel."

"I can't thank you enough, Dr. Rosie. I have never, ever had a birthday card. You are amazing."

Dr. Rosie stood and embraced Angel who could barely hold back her tears of joy.

"Are you expecting Officer Mitchell back, Angel?"

"Yes, I have an appointment with Dr. Jo. She sees me individually for counseling this afternoon and she will approve refills on my meds. Officer Mitchell will take me to her office."

"Okay, good. Let me know how it goes."

They looked up just as Officer Mitchell unlocked the door and waited for them to exit. Angel couldn't contain herself. "Officer Mitchell, look. Dr. Rosie brought me a birthday card." "That's lovely, Angel." She did not handcuff Angel. She slipped her an energy bar and said, "Nice to see you, Dr. Klein. Thank you for taking your time to visit Angel before her birthday."

"Glad to see you too. I will be back soon. And again, Angel, happy birthday." Rosie watched them walk down the hallway. Angel seemed to walking straighter with a quicker gait. Dr. Rosie sighed and walked to the elevator to go down where she would retrieve her identification and exit the building.

CHAPTER TWENTY-SEVEN

Angel's Journal Entry

What a treat to have Dr. Rosie come and see me again. It was nice to thank her in person and not in writing. Sometimes it is painful to relive the past, but she asks questions that require deep answers based on painful memories.

I wonder if there is a small chance that I can get out and work for Greg and Mikey. Mikey was so young when I left home. He was Rossi's favorite. He stayed behind when Mom and Greg went to the store. That was how Rossi controlled Mom. He knew she would never run off and leave Mikey behind. If it was just me, I don't think anything would have stopped her.

And then, Roger was not much better, except he had no favorites. Well, he did. He favored his own kid brother. That kid was so strong. He could pull me by my ponytail the length of a football field. Well, probably not that far. The path into the woods was narrow and wound around so much, he'd usually just drag me far enough not to be seen. I thought about screaming. Why didn't I?

I guess there was no one to hear me. Then in town, the guys who lived in the house with us drank, smoked, and played music so loud, and didn't care what happened to a little girl, anyhow.

I know I need to put all of that behind me including any anger and look forward to a better tomorrow. It's just hard to control my dreams and thoughts and to see anything different happening in my life.

Somehow, I feel like a phony. The words of encouragement I share with the other inmates are not sounding loudly in my own mind. I need to focus on my blessings, what I do have, like Chappy and Dr. Rosie, not what I lack. I have to remember that I always have a friend in Jesus and this world is not my final destination. I love watching shows about angels especially when they are people who died, usually tragically, and come back on a mission to save someone's life or help them believe in miracles. Well, good night, God.

***

Time to get up stupid. Those words came into Angel's head. She laid very still on her back and said out loud, "Stop it." She was taught that thought-stopping technique by Dr. Jo to remove negative thoughts from her mind. Dr. Jo said, "When the thought returns, and it will because you are human, say, "Stop it", slap your little face with the palm of your hand, and say, "I mean it." Then distract yourself with pleasant thoughts and visions before getting off your bunk.

That's exactly what Angel did before she slid her bare feet onto the cold cement floor and stretched her arms over her head. For relief of arthritic pain, she was taught by Dr. Jo to engage in stretching exercises prior to getting fully dressed. The idea of ever being fully dressed entered her thoughts fleetingly. Her one-piece orange jumpsuit with an elastic waist and black rubber flipflops with white cotton socks, when she had a clean pair, in no way fit the bill of being fully dressed.

Angel was dreading this day. It was not a workday, and it would be boring and drag on between meals. The weather was miserable. Sundays weren't as bad. There was Tom Brady and football. She turned her thoughts to tomorrow. Sunday. That is the way to distract myself, she thought.

Then Officer Mitchell showed up at her breakfast table. She took a seat across from her and said, "Trevor and Devon Gump, those lawyer fellows, have been approved and will be visiting you at 2:00. You might want to wash that stringy hair and clean those God-awful, greasy nails, Angel."

Suddenly Angel's mood lifted, and the day brightened with or without the sun. "That's great news. I can't believe this is really happening. I'm heading back to write in my journal and thank God for Dr. Rosie Klein. She has always told me the truth, good, bad, or otherwise. This proves she is truly an angel. Oh, for this occasion, I will enjoy the shower despite the cold water and a shampoo with that terrible, harsh soap. Could you watch me use the nail clippers. I promise not to hurt myself or anyone else if you let me clip these nails."

"I'd be glad to do that, Angel."

CHAPTER TWENTY-EIGHT

The Lawyers Visit

Travis and Devon Gump presented themselves at the counter where Kensington, the visitation officer sat. They signed the visitors log and showed their photo I.D.'s and their State Attorneys licenses. As instructed, they placed their billfolds, keys, belts, and briefcases on the conveyer belt and stepped through the security portal. They retrieved their items and walked toward the elevator. They had never interviewed an inmate at the Ohio Reformatory for Women. Most of their criminal clients were male. There had been some interviews and representation of women who were serving time in the county jails or being housed there until trial.

When the elevator door opened on the second floor, they were greeted by Officer Mitchell. She led them to a private interview room. They seated themselves, side by side, facing the door and waited for Angel Morgan to be brought down to them. It was uncomfortably cooler in the room than in the hall or on the elevator. There was a large glass window that was obvious. Other prisons had what appeared to be a large mirror, but officers could actually view and hear the interview from outside the room without being seen.

As Angel entered, both men stood and smiled. She took a seat putting her back to the window. "Good afternoon, Angel. I am Travis Gump, and this is my son, and business partner, Devon Gump. As you know, we have taken an interest in your case, based upon the information provided to us by Dr. Rosie Klein. Are you willing to speak with us?"

"Yes. I am very grateful that you drove all this way to see me. What should I call you guys?"

"We aren't very formal. Just call us Travis and Devon. That's fine. Would you sign a consent form to speak to us, confidentially of course?

"Sure. No problem." She took the pen that they slid over to her and quickly read the form. She signed it and slid it back to them.

"Why don't we start by you telling us why you are incarcerated here," Travis said.

"I was charged with four counts of murder, four counts of obstruction, and one count of accessory or something like that."

"Were you represented by an attorney?"

"Yes. Dan Singer represented me. He asked if I would testify against the two shooters. He said that if I did that, the Prosecutor would offer me a deal. So, I did. And it turned out that life in prison was the deal." Angel put her elbows on the table and leaned her head against her clenched fists.

"Did you realize that life in prison would be the deal, Angel?"

Angel looked down at her folded hands and answered, "Not exactly. I thought I was signing one count of murder and that I would possibly get released on good behavior at some point."

"We have access to all Dr. Rosie's records of your interviews with her and other materials she has obtained regarding your childhood, education and so on. Would you sign a release so that we can review all those records?"

"Yes. Glad to do that." Once more they slid a release form across the table to her. She signed it and handed it to Devon.

"Dr. Rosie has been an angel. She had me on her mind through the years and now we have become friends. I have a couple of other people who have been kind to me. Do you want to talk to them? They would talk to you."

"Sure," Travis said.

Devon took another form out of his briefcase and handed it to Angel. This was a general release form to allow the attorneys to speak to or read material from others who know Angel and with whom she has contact.

"Angel, your signature on this form permits us to speak with or read written materials from others who know you and have contact with you," Devon said.

"In that case, you should talk to my grandmother and my brothers and sister." She signed the form and handed it back."

"Okay. Does Dr. Klein have their contact information?" Travis asked.

"Yes, she has been in touch with them," Angel answered.

"You might not hear from us for a while. Don't think we have forgotten about you or that we aren't working in your behalf, okay?" Travis asked.

"Okay. Are you going to see Dr. Rosie? I have something I would like you to give her."

"As a matter of fact, we will be seeing her next weekend," Travis said.

Angel took a folded piece of unlined paper from her pocket. She handed it to Travis. She didn't explain what was written on it and he didn't unfold it or ask. He placed it into his briefcase. They both were wondering what it was that she was sending Dr. Rosie.

Officer Mitchell had been standing in view through the window for several minutes. She looked comfortable, not seeming to be in a hurry. The attorneys shook hands with Angel and stood up. Angel stood and turned toward the door. Officer Mitchell noticed she immediately unlocked the door. She allowed the men to pass by her. Again, she did not cuff Angel. She simply took her by the arm and escorted her down the hallway in the opposite direction of the men.

Once in the car, Travis and Devon decided to stop at a quaint Amish Café they had seen on the way up. It was just a few miles up the road. They took their briefcases with them with thoughts of discussing what they had experienced at the prison. They seated themselves as the little sign said and sat across from one another in a booth toward the back. Both had come to believe that when the weather is cold or damp, booths in the back of restaurants provide more protection from the elements.

"I know what you're thinking Dad," Devon said. "You are dying to know what Angel is sending to Rosie, aren't you? Tell the truth." Devon laughed and Travis pulled the paper out of his briefcase.

The waitress appeared wearing a name tag that said, Mable, and wool gloves with the fingers cut out. It confirmed that they were right when sitting toward the back of the café where it was warmer. She asked what they would like to drink.

"I'll have black coffee, Mable. How about you Devon?" Travis asked.

"Make it two. On second thought, I might need some sugar. Sugar and caffeine will keep me awake for the ride home."

"That's good, Devon, since I planned to ask you to drive," Travis laughed, and Devon frowned.

Mable returned with their drinks and took their orders. Both ordered chicken with noodles in heavy broth and homemade cherry pie.

"Okay, Devon." Travis unfolded the paper and smiled broadly. He placed it on the tabletop so Devon could see it. It was a Valentine's card for Dr. Rosie. Angel had drawn a large heart outlined in red but filled in with light pink. Within the boundaries it read, Happy Valentine's Day to my special angel. God loves you and so do I, Angel. In each corner of the page were two small pink hearts attached to one another.

"Not what I expected, Dad. Unbelievable. She is truly grateful for Rosie's friendship, isn't she?"

"Yes, she is. It makes me regret that we didn't ask to speak to Chaplain Caroline and Dr. Jo. Doing conference calls with them isn't the same as sitting down with them personally."

"It is a good reason to come back. Maybe we could drive Rosie up and observe Angel with her. If she is ever granted a parole hearing, this will give us an idea of how she comes off to others."

CHAPTER TWENTY-NINE

Week-End Guests

"Bucky, please get the door. It is Stella and Travis, and my hands are wet right this minute."

"No problem, Precious. I've got it," Bucky said with Willow wound around his ankles.

Rosie dried her hands and followed Bucky to the foyer.

"I'm so glad you two are able to come up for the weekend. Between Bucky's home basketball game tomorrow afternoon and dinner at our favorite steak house, it's going to be great," Rosie said as she embraced Stella.

Bucky took their coats and hung them on hooks above the bench. He and Travis followed the women into the great room where a crackling fire gained their attention.

"How simply lovely, Rosie," Stella said as she stood arm in arm, facing the fire, with her best friend. "It is toasty warm and helps thaw my bones. Really, the car was warm enough. Your log home is fantastic. Look up at the loft, Travis. Isn't that cool?"

Travis had followed Bucky to the stand-alone bar. They were coming toward the women with mugs of coffee mixed with Bailey's.

"We're going out to the car to bring the overnight bags and backpacks into the house," Bucky said.

There was a cheese tray with Summer Sausage, stuffed olives, crackers, red pepper hummus, and grapes on the coffee table. Travis and Stella sat on the loveseat while Bucky and Rosie sat across from them in their leather recliners. They all leaned forward and filled small plates with appetizers.

"Before I forget. I brought you something from Angel, Rosie," Travis said.

"Really? How nice of her and of you," Rosie said.

Travis handed her the paper that was folded in quarters. Rosie unfolded it and looked at the Valentine's card. Tears began to cloud her eyes. "Oh, my goodness, Bucky. Take a look at what she made me."

Rosie handed the card to Bucky. He rubbed Rosie's shoulder and handed it back. "How sweet," Bucky said.

CHAPTER THIRTY

Covid Strikes the Prison

The horn blasted for all the inmates to rise and shine, so the saying goes. There usually would be a trail of women heading to breakfast. Suddenly, on the loudspeaker, they were instructed to remain in their rooms. The warden announced that Dr. Jo, the prison medic, had identified a virus going around. Therefore, meals would be handed to them on trays. They were to have no direct contact with anyone outside or inside their rooms.

Angel had already been awake and propped up in her bed for forty-five minutes. As usual, she had prayed and written a few lines in her morning journal. She felt unusually warm but didn't notice a headache until her feet hit the cement floor. What in the world, she thought. Her stomach churned. She had not eaten in twelve hours so having stomach issues this early in the day was highly unusual. It is not as if she had eaten a greasy breakfast.

Officer Mitchell appeared at Angel's doorway. "Good morning, Angel. Your breakfast will not be brought to you. We need you to report to the sewing workshop for instructions. There will be no flags made in the foreseeable future. We have a new contract with the Government."

"Okay," Angel replied. She couldn't imagine what this was all about. As she leaned down to put her shoes on, she suddenly felt dizzy. She kept her head down between her knees and hoped the feeling would pass. It did. She tied her shoelaces and feeling wobbly, she followed Officer Mitchell to the sewing workshop.

Angel and the other sewers listened as their instructions were explained by Officer Strong. "The machines will be placed six feet apart by maintenance. You are not to touch anything anyone else has touched. You are not to talk to one another so that germs will not be transmitted in the air. We are facing a highly contagious virus, Covid 19. None of you have contracted it yet. If you think you have flu symptoms, please raise your hand to notify the supervisor of your shift. You will be taken to the clinic for evaluation. Covid symptoms may mock flu symptoms, but not exactly. Dr. Jo will make that determination.

If you are diagnosed with Covid, you will be quarantined for at least ten days, apart from your roommates. Your room will be sanitized and hopefully your roommates will not come down with it. We are setting up the infirmary area for all Covid inmates, like an emergency room. There will be curtains between each of your beds and a small chair to sit in, as well. If you are assigned there, take any personal items you want with you. You will not be permitted to leave the area."

Officer Strong continued the instructions. "If you are not ill, you may talk to your roommates if you wear a face mask and cover your mouth with your hand. Otherwise, you are to remain silent in your rooms and avoid getting close to any other inmate. You may wear your earphones to listen to recorded music, news, and so on. You can e-mail and watch televised events on your devices.

For those of you who are not sick, you will be sewing protective masks in twelve-hour shifts, six days a week. For your information, the government is providing these masks to medical personnel who are transporting or treating Covid patients. You will have breaks every two hours. Only one of you, at a time, is allowed to use the toilet. Raise your hand for that privilege. You will be expected to wipe down the toilet seat and sink prior to returning to your machine. There are sanitized paper towels in the bathroom. Any questions?"

No one responded. Officer Strong continued. "Lunch is at twelve-thirty. It will be eaten at your machine. In the mid-afternoon a nutrition bar and a bottle of water will be placed beside your sewing machine. Your shift will last late into the afternoon. Supper will be brought to your rooms on trays. Do not share food. Saving it is not allowed either.

Germs are spread from sneezing and coughing. It is advised that you sneeze or cough into your bent elbow and then immediately wash your hands and your arms. Sanitized moist issues will be placed on your food tray and each of you will receive a small pack when you begin and end your work shift. With your cooperation, ladies, we will get through this."

Everyone looked around, but no one said a word. There was dead silence, which was highly unusual. Usually, the inmates who worked together in the sewing workshop would chat with the inmates on either side of them and directly across. The sewing machine tables faced each other. Not this morning. Maintenance had already placed them six feet apart in all directions.

Angel raised her hand to get the attention of the officer in charge. She didn't want to spread whatever she had, Covid or not. Officer Strong immediately noticed and walked over to where Angel sat.

"I am not feeling well. I woke up with a headache and felt dizzy as soon as I leaned down to put on my shoes."

"Okay, Angel. Let's go to the clinic and let Dr. Jo look at you. You recently got over the flu, right?" Angel nodded yes. Officer Strong slipped on her mask and gloves and took Angel's arm. She walked slowly beside her to the clinic.

"Dr. Jo has a way of testing for Covid. She will have instant results. Better safe than sorry as far as spreading it, but more importantly, getting you feeling better. It might just be a bug of some kind." Officer Strong thought that this was probably serious because Angel Morgan never called off sick from a shift

Dr. Jo was sitting at her desk. "Good morning, Dr. Jo," As you can see, Angel Morgan is not feeling well," Officer Strong said.

"Please sit down, Angel. You look very pale. I will test for Covid and listen to your chest and lungs." Officer Strong left the clinic and Dr. Jo began her examination.

Twenty minutes later, Dr. Jo confirmed that Angel tested positive for Covid. "Sure, enough the results were Covid," Dr. Jo explained to Angel.

"Angel, I will call Chaplain Caroline and she will be glad to get the personal items that you want from your room. She will sanitize them and bring them to you. What exactly would you like to have?" Dr. Jo asked.

"I need my Women's Devotional Bible, my Worry, Fret, and Fear book that Dr. Rosie wrote, my two brown leather journals and my pens. For now, is it okay if I sleep? I can hardly keep my eyes open, Dr. Jo." Angel kicked her shoes off and laid down on the little bed.

"Absolutely. Rest is what you need. And liquids." Dr. Jo handed Angel a bottle of water and two Tylenol capsules for her headache. She placed a blanket over Angel. She then disposed of the rubber gloves she was wearing and put on a fresh pair. She took a sip of coffee from her insulated cup. She knew days were to become much longer as she treats the victims of this viral infection.

CHAPTER THIRTY-ONE

A Slow Recovery

Angel awakened with a start and wondered what time it was and even what day it was. She had slept day and night except when an officer awakened her every eight hours to drink water or to eat a small, bland meal. Breakfast, lunch, and supper were basically the same, toast, a hardboiled egg, yogurt, a banana or an apple, and hot tea. It really didn't matter. She couldn't taste or smell anything. She was relieved that for the first time, she finally didn't wake up with a headache. It was also a blessing that according to Dr. Jo, her lungs were clear.

She was told she could return to the sewing workshop once her symptoms remitted, and she could stay alert for at least a couple hours. The good news was that she was going to be promoted to a supervisory position. This meant her sore joints would have time to heal. She was surprised when Officer Howard, the Assistant Warden, sent a written message to her that read that her work history supported a promotion. It would commence immediately upon her return to work and the pay would be retroactive to the beginning of her sick leave.

Sick pay? Angel couldn't believe she would receive sick pay. And what would the new position pay? Would it be an hourly wage, daily, or weekly? Was there overtime available?

The bad news was that there could be no visitors or phone calls during the course of the pandemic. Dr. Jo told her that Covid-19 was known as a pandemic because it has spread, literally, worldwide. People are dying. Angel prayed that no one she knew would succumb that way to the disease. Distance would still be observed, and meals eaten at the sewing machines or in the inmates' rooms.

Just when Angel was beginning to meet with professional people and experiencing hope for her future, this stupid virus caused a setback. When Dr. Jo arrived to take her temperature and blood pressure, she said, "Dr. Jo. Could you please make sure that Dr. Rosie and the two lawyers, Travis and Devon Gump, are informed that I am sick, we are locked down, and they can't visit or receive calls from me?"

"No problem, Angel. I know how much it has meant to you to have Dr. Rosie and the lawyers take an interest in you and in your case. It's great to see your spirits lifted by your relationship with Rosie Klein."

"Well, Dr. Jo, with the attorneys looking into my case, it gives me hope of a life outside of these bars." Angel's voice sounded more positive.

CHAPTER THIRTY-TWO

Bad News

Rosie saw there was a call coming in from the Ohio Reformatory for Women. "Hello, "Rosie said.

"Hi, Rosie. This is Daisy Marigold. I'm' calling to tell you that Covid-19 has put our entire facility on quarantine."

"Thank you, Daisy, for notifying me. Is Angel, okay?"

"She came down with it and is serving at least ten days in quarantine. All the inmates, sick or not, are quarantined until further notice. The staff are tested every shift to be sure they aren't bringing the virus in. That is how it had to have gotten here. Either staff or venders that deliver produce etc."

"Is her case serious?"

"The first five days she slept the majority of the time. We made sure she was awakened to drink water and take Vitamin C, Zinc, and Tylenol."

"Are her symptoms severe?"

"She has no congestion or breathing issues. She has a low-grade fever and complains of a severe headache, like a vice behind her head and neck. She is finally eating small meals and resting without falling sleep. You know how much Angel enjoys reading her Women's Devotional Bible and writing in her journals. She did none of that during the first five days. For brief periods, she has been seen reading and writing again."

"That's good news. Tell her we'll be praying for her."

"I will. Just wanted to be sure that you knew she was sick and that you don't come up and be turned away. Plus, phone calls are prohibited indefinitely. It is believed that anything we touch can transmit the virus. Liquid sanitizer is located everywhere, counters, bathrooms, copy machines. We also use wet, sanitized, disposable towels for our hands and surfaces."

"I appreciate your call, Daisy."

"I have a favor to ask," Daisy said.

"Okay."

"Please let the attorneys know they can't communicate or visit so they don't make a trip for nothing. Mail delivery directly to our facility has been discontinued. All mail or packages delivered by USPS, U.P.S., FedEx, or any other service, are being sent to a prison distribution center in Youngstown. From there, a courier will eventually deliver the sanitized mail. Letters will be removed from the envelopes, sanitized, and delivered. I guess what I am saying is not to expect Angel to receive anything in a timely manner. Eventually, it will arrive."

"I'll write to her tomorrow. You can tell her that we talked and that I am writing."

"Certainly. Regardless of what her future holds, it is nice to know she has you in her life. Her grandmother can no longer travel and likely suffers from dementia. Phone calls are monitored, and their conversations are sometimes convoluted. Grandma calls her Amanda by mistake. That sort of thing. This depresses Angel. It is better for her to rely on sweet memories of their past relationship."

"Please keep me posted as to Angel's recovery and let me know when the circumstances change. Hopefully, by Spring, the virus will have passed, and I can visit her again."

"I will gladly do that. Bye Rosie."

***

"Bucky, where are you?"

"I'm in the office. Do you need me?" He unwound Willow from his ankles and got up from his desk chair. Rosie stood in his doorway, shoulders slumped, looking discouraged.

"Just wanted to tell you that Daisy Marigold, Angel's case manager just called to alert me that Covid-19 has gotten into the women's reformatory. Many, including Angel, are sick."

"No kidding. Is she seriously ill?"

"She has overcome the worst of it. I guess it knocked her for a loop for about five days."

"It must feel like being punished for a crime you didn't cause or commit. I suppose they're all quarantined 24/7."

"Yup," Rosie said with a sad tone of voice. Bucky approached her and gave her a hug.

CHAPTER THIRTY-THREE

Unexpected Visit

Chappy, wearing a face mask, stood quietly at the entrance to Angel's room. Angel looked up from her writing and smiled. She said, "I sensed you were standing there, Chappy. I guess you heard I was pretty sick, right?" Chappy did not approach Angel. Chappy knew that even with a mask, staying distant from others was needed for protection.

"Yes, Angel. I did. All my groups and classes have been postponed while we are under quarantine. Have I told you how much I enjoy you co-leading a Beautiful Life? Those young women have had anything but a beautiful life. When they hear your story, they gain new insight into how to lead a drug-free, crime-free life. They see what poor choices can result in. They also eliminate that victim mentality that always led them to feeling helpless and hopeless."

"I know. I feel so sorry for them, particularly the young ones. Being here for a year at eighteen would be so hard to handle. The only terrible thing I didn't experience as a juvenile run away was prostitution. Thank God I wasn't trafficked and didn't have a pimp like some of them do," Angel said.

"That was a blessing. As for those young women, when they are released, they need to be transported to a new community to start new lives. Most of their pimps have been arrested, but their drug dealers will be looking for them to collect money for drugs they were given to sell," Chappy said.

"I just received a letter from Kaitlin. Remember her from last year, Chappy?"

"I certainly do."

"She found her aunt, and she is living with her on Hilton Head Island. I made three friends who met on that Island. One attended a music boarding school on a nearby Island, Baden Island. Then there was April who scooped ice cream at an outdoor shopping square and was in love with a guy named Sam, who just got out of the marines. Sam sang and played the guitar. April and Sam were orphans together in Toledo before he joined the marines. She was younger than Sam.

They were just on Hilton Head Island for the summer. April and Sam planned to get jobs in Toledo in the fall. They told Song to apply to the University of Toledo to study music. She ended up with a scholarship," Angel said.

"Are you still in touch?"

"Not exactly. One is here with me. You know her. My co-defendant, Song."

"How did you meet?" Chappy inquired with a sympathetic voice.

"She fell for the wrong guy her second year and stopped going to classes. She lived in a house with James and Marcus and then they invited April and Sam to move in with them. That was the group that ended up in our little "downtown posse." That is what the cops and news media called us.

James, Song and I are serving the same sentences. They are the ones who get to have a parole hearing because they became sentenced as adults when they were minors."

"You mentioned Marcus. What happened to him? Was he one of the shooters?"

"Marcus was the leader. He got the death penalty and was put to death about seven years ago. His appeals didn't work. You knew that I testified against Marcus and James, didn't you?"

"Yes. I didn't know their names. How about the other two, Sam and April?"

She turned her back to Chappy and stood silently. Finally, she took a deep breath and turned around. She quickly took a seat on the edge of her bed, hung her head, and clasped her hands. Her voice broke as she answered, "They're dead."

"I am so sorry, Angel. What happened to them?"

"They were executed by two of our gang. The two guys that did all the killing, Marcus, and James, thought that Sam and April were going to tell. That was the furthest thing from the truth. And get this, Chappy, the three of us were ordered to get out of the car, walk twenty paces, put our hands behind our backs and get on our knees. I was spared. Sam and April were not. I prayed to God to save me, and a miracle happened. For days, I cried privately for my two friends."

"Oh, my gosh. That's horrible," Chappy responded in a soft, compassionate voice. "Tragic story. Where was Song during this execution?"

"She was told to stay in the back seat with me and for us to keep our heads down. She was James' girlfriend and he protected her. Song and I didn't know for sure who pulled the triggers. We assumed Marcus and James each shot one of our friends. The sound of the bullets seemed, how do you say it, simultaneous?"

"How in the world did April and Sam get involved with the others?"

"They worked for an old man named George who owned a bar with an apartment above it. He helped them when they were children in the orphanage. He provided Christmas and birthday gifts and circus tickets for all the orphans. They knew he had a soft heart. They lived above the bar and cleaned it every night after it closed. George suspected they were doing drugs. Sure enough. He had to fire them and evict them. Song and April had kept up their friendship after the Summer at Hilton Head Island. Song invited them to live in a vacant house with her and James and Marcus."

"Were the men homeless?"

"Yes. It was getting cold. The first snow had already come and gone. The people who owned the house were in Florida for the winter. The problem was that they turned off the electricity and the water so the pipes wouldn't freeze. There was a space heater in the unattached garage behind the house. There was an alley entrance into the garage. I think they ran an extension cord to the garage next door where there was power. Most of the time, we sat out there. The men gambled, drank, and smoked pot with other men who stopped by every night."

"All the women in group with you, Angel, are aware that you were involved in a serious crime spree, but they don't know all these details and your hardship. When you feel strong enough, I would like you to tell your story about how based on these tragic events, you came to have a personal relationship with God. Can you do that?"

"Yes, Chappy. I am writing about it and maybe it would be good if I share some of my writing. It could encourage them to write their feelings and thoughts. Don't you think?"

"That's a great idea. And we can start back up with our praise dancing as a means of gratitude and expression of faith. Between Covid-19 quarantine and not having you, it has been discontinued. You are a terrific dancer, displaying fantastic emotion."

"Wow, I didn't know you felt that way." Angel stood up, wiped her tears, brushed her hair from her eyes, and smiled.

"Bye, Angel. Eat more than you have been, so you don't lose too much weight and can gain back your strength. When you go back to the sewing workshop, you will need to be strong. In order to meet the production deadlines, mandated by the federal government contract, it involves twelve-hour shifts. That way we will provide two million protective masks and twenty thousand disposable gowns.

There are breaks of course. I think on Saturdays they only work six hours. I made sure they don't work on Sunday so they can worship and rest. I can tell you they are very tired. And now, I will let you rest."

Chappy really wanted to reach out and hug Angel, but because of Covid , she restrained herself.

"Bye, Chappy. I can't thank you enough for stopping to check on me. Tell them I will eat regular meals now."

"Okay. Sounds good. Let me know if you need anything else."

Angel blew Chappy a kiss which brought a wave and a smile from Chappy.

CHAPTER THIRTY-FOUR

Interview with F.B.I.

"Mrs. Marigold, this is Liza Cunningham. I am an agent with the F.B.I. and I would like to make an appointment to speak to you, your chaplain, and one of your inmates, Angel Morgan?"

"Can you tell me what this is in reference to? We are just coming off a lengthy quarantine period due to Covid. The Warden is cautious about our exposure because he doesn't want the officers, staff, or inmates to come down with it again."

"It is about a former inmate, Cindy Tipton. I would be willing to take a Covid test and meet with you off the grounds. Would that work and could you suggest a suitable place?"

"That sounds good, Agent Cunningham. We could meet at the Amish Café about two miles from the reformatory . I usually have time available on Friday afternoons."

"Okay. I just need time, date, and an address, please."

"Can I e-mail it to you? I don't have the address handy right now."

"Sure. My private e-mail address is LC917@gmail.com."

"By the way, why do you want to talk to Angel Morgan? She has been seriously ill between the flu and Covid. It is unlikely that you can see her. Possibly, a video conference call would work.

"It has come to our attention that Bonnie Tipton's sister, Cindy, who was incarcerated at your facility for having sex with a minor. She was there for about three years, and we are hoping she may have information regarding the location of her brother and sister, Bonnie and Clyde Tipton. Cindy could have inadvertently gotten information from Angel Morgan that assisted them in committing another crime, against Dr. Rosie Klein, and then fleeing the country."

"Good heavens. What do you mean? Information from Angel? At this point in her life, Angel wouldn't harm a fly."

"As I said, the victim was Dr. Rosie Klein, Mrs. Marigold. Just overhearing Angel talk about her would have been enough for Bonnie and her brother to search her out."

"Is Dr. Klein hurt?"

"No. Bonnie and her brother are suspects in the poisoning of Dr. Klein's dog. Cindy knew they were out for revenge because of Dr. Klein's intervention in their trafficking ring. This led to their arrest over twenty years ago."

"Are they in custody?"

"No. They have violated their parole by leaving the State of Michigan and likely sneaking out of the country. They are on the run. They may be in Canada. That was where they trafficked young girls."

"Well, I will speak to Angel about it before we meet. She may not have actually met Cindy Tipton. They could have been eating a meal in the same vicinity or walking around near one another in the courtyard."

"That's so true. Thank you for inquiring. It also could have been another inmate talking about how lucky Angel is to have Dr. Klein as a pen pal."

"They have become quite close. Dr. Klein has restored hope for Angel."

"I know. I am acquainted with Dr. Klein, and she speaks very highly of you and Angel and Chaplain Caroline. Is there a chance that Chaplain Caroline may know of Cindy Tipton?"

"Could be. I will check with her."

"I will wait to hear the final arrangements for our meeting. Thank you for your cooperation."

"You are welcome. I will send the e-mail in the next fifteen minutes. Have a nice day."

***

"Good morning, Angel," Mrs. Marigold said as she stood in the doorway of Angel's room wearing her protective mask.

Angel looked up from her Bible and answered with a quizzical look, "Good morning, Mrs. Marigold. Should I put my mask on?"

"No. It won't be necessary. How are you feeling?"

"So much better. I am beginning to taste some food again. And based on the odor from my sneakers, I am smelling stuff, good or bad." Angel laughed.

"That's good. They certainly have missed you in the sewing workshop. The reason I stopped by is to ask you about a former inmate. Did you ever know an inmate by the name of Cindy Tipton? She would be about ten years older than you."

"Let me think. Cindy Tipton. Did she have red hair and a lot of wrinkles around her lips from smoking, probably?"

"I'm not sure. I wasn't her case manager. I never met her. An FBI agent inquired about her and whether you might have known her."

"Well, she didn't sew. That's for sure. I think she worked in the kitchen. She never smiled. She wore a hairnet, but I could see her stringy red hair hanging on her forehead. Come to think of it, I haven't noticed her in a few months. Why is the FBI interested in her?"

"Apparently, her sister Bonnie and brother, Clyde, continue to be seen as a threat to Dr. Rosie Klein. And now, Bonnie and Clyde have violated parole. It is believed they have left the United States. They're on the run."

"Oh my gosh. What did they do to Dr. Rosie? That scares me to death."

"They lured her dog to the gate at the entrance to the driveway to their house. They poisoned him. They are suspects. It has not been proven in a court of law. Meanwhile, they have violated parole by coming to Ohio from Michigan. Their vehicle has been identified as being in Ohio."

"How awful." Angel wiped a tear from her cheek. "Dr. Rosie and her husband, Bucky, loved that dog. I think his name was Champ and he replaced Jocko and Luke who were their previous dogs."

"The Agent, Liza Cunningham, would like to speak with you on a video conference. Would that be agreeable? Meanwhile, you can think about how Cindy Tipton possibly gained information about Dr. Klein from listening to your conversation, perhaps? Or the two of you may have talked in a class and you mentioned your relationship with Dr. Klein?"

"I don't see how that could have happened with her working in the kitchen. I don't remember her in chapel or in any groups or classes. But

I will rack my brain to figure that out. I know we never had a one-on-one conversation, let alone about my personal relationships."

"I am meeting with Agent Cunningham on Friday afternoon. I will get back to you about setting up a video conference call. Take care of yourself. You are missed in the sewing workshop."

"I know. I think I will test negative very soon. It has been nice being back in my room instead of in the clinic where just curtains separated me from the other sick women. My roommates made that happen by volunteering to be in another room temporarily."

"That is nice. I'm sure it is better to have privacy when you don't feel well."

"It is easier to pray and read when I'm by myself. That way I am not distracted and not looking rude to the other person."

"Bye, Angel."

"Bye, Mrs. Marigold. If you speak with Dr. Klein, tell my angel that I'm doing better. She is so sweet; she is probably worried about me."

"I'm sure she is. Will do."

Mrs. Marigold walked to the chapel to speak to Chaplain Caroline. Tomorrow she would speak to the Deputy Warden about who was Cindy Tipton's last case manager. Mrs. Marigold knew that he was in Columbus today at a meeting for the State of Ohio, Deputy Wardens.

CHAPTER THIRTY-FIVE

Staff Memories

"Hi Caroline," Daisy Marigold said, as she approached the podium where Chaplain Caroline stood.

"Well, hello, Daisy. What brings you to the chapel today?"

"I was hoping you'd be here alone. I need some help, not of a spiritual nature. Did you know Cindy Tipton? She spent three years here and I was not her case manager. In fact, I replaced her case manager, but Cindy wasn't assigned to me. She was recently released, and the FBI is investigating her sister and brother, Bonnie, and Clyde Tipton. They hope to locate Cindy and gain some valuable information about them."

"Cindy Tipton? Huh." Chaplain Caroline asked. "I wish I could help you, but in the years I have been here, she did not participate in any classes that I offered or attend worship services on Wednesday or Sunday."

"An FBI agent by the name of Liz Cunningham is going to have a video conference call with Angel Morgan to see if she knew Cindy. Supposedly, Bonnie Tipton and her brother are suspected of poisoning Dr. Klein's dog as revenge," Daisy said.

"Revenge? What could that sweet lady ever have done that would cause them to want nasty revenge like that?"

"She played a part in investigating and apprehending them twenty or so years ago, and that led to lengthy sentences they both served for sex trafficking. Agent Cunningham told me she thinks that somehow Cindy, while serving time here for having sex with a minor, found out where Dr. Klein works and lives. She may have gained this information by overhearing a conversation Angel had with an inmate. Though I just spoke with Angel, and she doesn't recall any conversation with anyone outside or in the cafeteria, about her relationship with Dr. Klein. She told me that Cindy worked in the kitchen behind the serving counters and was never on the floor," Daisy said.

"How awful to poison a dog for revenge. Nice family that Cindy belongs to. Do you think Dr. Klein's life is in danger?" Caroline asked.

"Not right now. Agent Cunningham said the Tipton's likely managed to sneak out of the country. They violated the conditions of their parole, and they are on the run. They must have gotten an inkling that they were being watched. Cindy could be the key to finding them."

"You might want to speak to Dr. Jo. Every inmate, at one time or another, passes through her clinic. She is likely to have an entire medical history on Cindy Tipton."

"That's a great idea. I will do that."

"Good luck. I can tell you this. If Cindy's sister Bonnie trafficked children and the inmates knew it, Cindy had to be extremely unpopular. She might have seen Dr. Jo for injuries sustained by angry inmates," Caroline said.

"I never thought of that. You are so right. These women who are tragically, involuntarily separated from their own children would hate tolerating an inmate who deprived parents of their kids."

"Here comes a group of ladies that I call my prayer warriors," Chaplain Caroline said.

"Well, ask them to pray that Bonnie and her brother are returned to prison on new charges."

"You don't think she would end up here, do you?"

"I don't know how the law works. Their parole violation is in Michigan, but their poisoning of Dr. Rosie's dog occurred in Ohio. I suspect they would be returned to Michigan. Unless they commit a crime where they are hiding and are arrested there."

***

Daisy Marigold entered the clinic and walked up to the receptionist desk where a rather young, attractive inmate was seated. She wore a magnetic name tag that identified her as a receptionist for Dr. Jo.

"How can I help you, Mrs. Marigold?"

"Hi, Trinity." Mrs. Marigold recalled speaking to Trinity several times when she came to her office to request a part-time job in the medical field. She had been a nurse but lost her license and her freedom when she became addicted to painkillers and passed them on to friends.

"I am hoping to speak briefly with Dr. Jo. Is she busy?" Daisy noticed that the door to the examining room was ajar.

"I am sure you can knock and go on in. She just hung up from a conference call with two other prison doctors. And thank you again for recommending me to Dr. Jo. This job has been extremely fulfilling. After I screwed up royally, I never thought I would be working in the medical field again."

"You deserved the chance. As your case manager, I spoke to previous employers, and they all thought you were extremely competent and that your personality suits being in a helping profession. I was told that patients who were Police officers, firemen, EMTs, and first responders all respected you."

"I had no idea they saw me that way. I let them down. I let my family down, I let myself down. And when I am released, although I can't regain my license, I want to help other health care workers who struggle with depression, and addiction." She took a tissue out of her sleeve and wiped the tears from her eyes.

Dr. Jo walked into the reception area and stood beside the desk. "To what do we owe this honor?" She asked.

"There is an important matter I would like to speak to you about," Daisy said.

"Come on in. I was just about to have a mug of hot chai tea latte. Would you care to have one?"

"Sure. I am usually a black coffee drinker. This will be a treat. I think my grandkids drink lattes."

Dr. Jo handed Daisy the mug she was holding with hot, frothy milk on top. She proceeded to make another latte for herself. Then she sat on the edge of her desk because there was only one other chair in the room, along with an examining table. Daisy seated herself in front of Jo, looked up at her and explained."

"I came to ask you if you knew or treated Cindy Tipton. She was released after spending three years here for sex with a minor."

"I do know Cindy. I re-filled a prescription for pills she uses to treat her Herpes. She has occasional episodes or outbursts of lesions. I heard that back in California she caught her husband cheating with his ex-wife. As it turns out he had given Herpes to Cindy. For revenge his ex-wife infected him deliberately. Supposedly, he was unaware that he had the disease." They both laughed.

"Oh, my gosh. Can you imagine that?" Daisy asked.

"Then the husband mysteriously drowned in a freak automobile accident. His car plummeted nose down, into a lake, after missing a treacherous curve in the narrow road. It was in the hills above the city of Berkeley, California. He worked for Libby Labs pharmaceutical company. Until she divorced him, they lived on Virginia and Ninth Street which was a short walk to the Lab at Virginia and Sixth. Cindy was managing a couple of rental houses that they owned."

"How did Cindy end up in Ohio?"

"After her husband's accidental death, she moved to Toledo to be near her ailing mother and brother, John, who was also divorced and living with their mother. Cindy's sister, Karen lived nearby and was dedicated to their mother. The kid Cindy had sex with mowed her mother's lawn and lived next door to her. The parents of this fifteen-year-old boy pressed charges."

"While she was in Toledo her brother, John, took a trip out West to put Cindy's rentals up for sale. She was awarded the houses in the divorce decree. He became a person of interest in the death of her ex-husband, but it was ruled accidental."

"Did you treat Cindy for anything else?"

"Yes. Occasionally she received burns on her hands or arms from hot grease that splattered on her in the kitchen. And she also suffered from menopause. She had hot flashes at night and excessive sweating in the daytime. Those symptoms, coupled with urinary tract infections, irregular bleeding, and depression brought her in to see me at least a handful of times."

"Do you know anything about her brother, Clyde? He was in prison, too? Did their mother visit them?"

"After their mother died, Cindy came into the office and burst into tears. She said that her mother died and her sister Karen, blamed her. Apparently, Karen wrote Cindy and told her their mother died of a broken heart because Cindy, Bonnie, and Clyde turned out to be hoodlums."

"Do you have any idea where Karen, Cindy, or John might live or how Agent Cunningham can get ahold of them? Maybe one of them has been contacted by Bonnie and Clyde."

"No. Cindy didn't list anyone as next of kin in the clinic. You might check your records that would date back to when she was first incarcerated."

"I will do that. Thanks for the Latte and the interesting story of Cindy Tipton."

"You are welcome. I will be so glad when this Covid pandemic passes," Jo said. "The women are so antsy being couped up all day. The only ones who are not quarantined and healthy have jobs in the sewing workshop, the kitchen, or the laundry room. It is extremely important that the inmates have sanitized, clean uniforms and bedding."

"Daisy Marigold stood and said, "I will let Agent Cunningham know everything you told me about Cindy and her family. She may want to get in touch. You will like her. She is friendly and professional."

Dr. Jo smiled and nodded affirmatively. She put her cup down and stood to escort Daisy back to the waiting room. Trinity was still sitting at the desk. She was handing paperwork to an inmate who wanted to be seen by Dr. Jo. Trinity looked up and thought about how much she admired Dr. Jo and Mrs. Marigold. She vowed to herself that she would not let them or anyone down again.

CHAPTER THIRTY-SIX

Communication Resumes

Hi Dr. Rosie,

I am finally over Covid and am returning to work on Monday. I am sorry I didn't e-mail you sooner, but my blood pressure has been up, and I have not felt well. How is your volunteer work going with those men at the Christian half-way house? That is very beautiful that you teach at that place. They are so lucky to have you teaching them anger management. Those first years, my time here would have passed so much easier if I had anger classes. Not only that, but those guys need to know you love them and will not abandon them, reject them, or disown them like my mother did to me.

Thank the men for praying for me. I need all the prayers I can get. And I feel it when others pray for me. Feel free to tell them my story. I wish I could write a book about it. You are welcome to use it in a book. I think I told you before that I tell my story to the women who are coming in. I tell them it is so easy to get caught up, like you can be in a car and someone you are with goes in and robs the store and you don't even know it until it is too late. I have helped a lot of people by telling them my sentence. I have had people write and tell me that I saved them. Of course, it isn't true. Only God saves you, but I direct them to Jesus, and our chaplain, Chappy Caroline.

It took me a long time here to figure out my purpose. That is, to save and help others. I am running out of power. Good night. Sleep with the angels. You are one of them.

Thank you.
Angel

CHAPTER THIRTY-SEVEN

Rosie Moves Ahead

"Hey Bucky. I got the sweetest e-mail message from Angel. The Covid restrictions have been lifted and she is over the nasty virus. The problem is that she has blood pressure problems and migraines. I want you to read it."

"Okay. I was just about to get us a glass of Shiraz and some goat cheese with blueberry topping and crackers. Does that sound good to you?"

"Of course. You are such a dear man and you obviously read my thoughts well."

Bucky came into the family room where Rosie sat in front of the fire in her favorite brown leather recliner. Her legs were stretched out and Willow was cuddled in her lap. He placed the appetizers and wine on the small oak table between their chairs. He reached over, took Rosie's laptop from her outstretched arms, and sat down in his matching lounge chair to read Angel's message. As soon as he began, the expression on his face went from a smile to a look of frustration.

Rosie put Willow down and went out to the kitchen to pop a veggie pizza in the oven.

"What are you going to do, Rosie," Bucky called out to her. She really wants her story told and she praises you to high heaven for your work with the guys at Casa Hope Residential Treatment House."

"If I could get the Governor to commute her sentence. Assuming you agree, she could stay here with us for three to six months. It would give her time to develop a plan for her future and to accompany me when I teach anger management at Casa Hope. The men would enjoy meeting her since they have been praying for her release. During that time, we could help her get her driver's license. She could get a permit and use one of our cars to practice driving and parking. Then there are several Christian women's homes that would gladly allow her to stay a year. But I must say, it sounds as if she would rather become part of her brothers' lives as soon as possible."

"That's a great plan. I don't object at all. She would love Willow. We could buy her a sewing machine and encourage our friends to have her mend or alter their clothes to save money while she's here," Bucky said.

"Let's not put the cart before the horse. The Governor has not responded to the letter you sent him, right? Without his or someone's intervention, none of this plan can come to fruition."

"Terrible that Travis and Devon's representation was interrupted by Covid. I will call Travis tomorrow and tell him that Angel survived, and she goes back to work on Monday. The only thing is that visitors are still not permitted," Rosie said.

"They have some investigative work to complete anyhow, don't they?" Bucky said.

"Yes. They want to follow up with Angel's brothers to see if she is truly welcome to work in their ice cream/coffee shop and if there is a place where she can live."

"If her information is accurate, after her three months with us, we can drive her up there. That would be fun wouldn't it, Precious?" Bucky took Rosie's long stem glass to refill it with more dark red wine for "medicinal purposes" and chuckled to himself.

***

"Good morning. Gump Law Offices," Stella Gump said with a jovial voice.

"Hi Stella. This is your old roomie, Rosie. Are you still filling in for your husband's receptionist on this cold, Friday morning?"

"Yes, sorry I neglected to tell you when we were together, that the receptionist is Brenda, our son, Devon's wife. Remember how pregnant she was when you met?"

"Yes. Lovely though. Radiant really. Were we radiant when we were nine months pregnant?"

"At this point the only description of Brenda is impatient," Stella answered with a comical tone.

She is two weeks overdue. If she doesn't go into labor by midnight, she will be induced at the hospital in the morning. They had a midwife lined up who has been right there beside her throughout the pregnancy. Unfortunately, the little one has not decided to face this world of ours yet. And as far as radiant, I recall that you looked it, but I appeared more ragged."

She heard Rosie's laughter. "I will connect you with Travis. Devon is at home lending moral support and rubbing her back. Nice to talk to you Rosie. We had fun together, didn't we?"

"Yes, we did. I predict we will get together often now that our husbands enjoy each other's company."

"Rosie," this is Travis. I was thinking about you. I have a conference call scheduled tomorrow with Greg and Mike, Angel's brothers."

"That's great news. I was calling to tell you that she emailed me to say she has gotten over Covid and is going back to work on Monday. The only problem left is that visitors are not allowed. And the inmates still can't use the phones as a precaution because germs might be spread. You can e-mail her. That's what I plan to do."

"How about I get back to you once I talk to her brothers. We don't want to proceed if living with them and working for them is just a pipe dream. Right?"

"Yes. I agree. I might hold off writing her until I hear back from you. Then I will share the first part of the plan with you once she is released. It will remain between you, Devon, Bucky, Stella, and me."

"Oh, wait. Devon is on the phone and wants to speak to you. I'll put him on speaker phone."

"Hi Rosie. Brenda went into labor and is in the bedroom with the midwife, Maria. I think we will have a new addition to our family tonight. We would like to ask if you and Bucky would consider being god parents to our son or daughter. We wanted to be surprised and not know the gender ahead of time."

"Of course, we would be honored to be godparents. Let us know when our first godchild arrives."

"Thank you. Brenda has been on me to make this request since the first time she met you. It takes a lot off my plate to know you will do it."

"Let us know when our first godchild arrives."

127

"I will. And tell our godchild, we are looking forward to making her or him a superb athlete, as well as a God loving child."

CHAPTER THIRTY-EIGHT

The Search Continues

Mrs. Marigold returned to her office and began to review the intake forms completed by Cindy Tipton upon her admission to prison. She listed the names of her two brothers, Clyde and John, and two sisters, Karen and Bonnie, with no known addresses or telephone numbers. As to who to contact in an emergency she provided one name with contact information. The name was John Grafton. His relationship to her said, Uncle. His address was in Phillipsburg, St. Martin.

"That's it," she said out loud. She picked up the phone to contact Dr. Klein.

Dr. Klein heard her phone ring, and quickly went to the kitchen island where her phone lay. She answered and was pleasantly surprised to hear Mrs. Marigold say, "Hi Rosie. I hope I am not disturbing you this late in the evening. I have news to share."

"Hi, Daisy. You're still at work? Bucky and I were relaxing in front of the fire. No problem, at all."

"I felt the need to research for you. I have information regarding the possible whereabouts of Bonnie and Clyde Tipton. You may want to pass it along to Agent Cunningham."

"Great. I will. How did you come by this information?"

"I was talking to Dr. Jo, our medic, and she told me she treated Cindy Tipton, get this, for Herpes. She knew a little about Cindy's background and advised me to look at the intake forms to see if she listed next of kin. And, if she listed someone as her emergency contact."

"Did she?"

"Yes. She is alienated from her sister, Karen, who blamed her along with Bonnie and Clyde for their mother's death. Broken heart, Karen told her. She has an older brother, John, named after their uncle, who seems to have been protective of her. Her brother went to California to sell her houses after her cheating husband's accidental death. Of course,

Bonnie and Clyde were in prison. So, she named John Grafton as her emergency contact. It said the relationship is that he is her mother's brother, her uncle. Get this, Rosie, he lives in Saint Martin."

"Really? Is there a phone number?"

"You have to dial one before the area code and number for an international call. Yes, she listed his number and address in Phillipsburg, a town on the Dutch side of the island."

"I will turn this information over to Sheriff Holland and Agent Cunningham. They will probably call the siblings, Karen, Cindy, and John prior to attempting to reach Uncle John."

"I tend to agree."

"Thank you, Daisy. You amaze me with your investigative mindset. Hope to see you soon. I will be back down to visit Angel in June and perhaps we can have dinner in Marysville."

"That would be great. You can stay with me if you want to remain overnight. Coming all that way you are permitted to see Angel on two consecutive days."

"That is a great idea. After my visit, I plan to head down to Dayton to visit my mother and stepfather. Bucky will not be coming this trip. He has recruiting obligations."

"Let me know what happens, Rosie. Stay safe."

"That's how Angel ends her letters to me because the world was never safe for her. Tell her we talked, and I am thinking of her."

***

"Good morning, Sheriff," Rosie said. She took her first cup of coffee to her chair in front of the fireplace. Bucky had stoked the fire earlier in the morning and added a couple more logs. He had an early meeting with the coaches of several different teams.

"Good morning, Rosie. What prompts you to call? Everything okay out there?"

"Yes. We are fine. I have news to share with you and Liza. Daisy Marigold, Angel's case manager, tracked down the siblings of Bonnie and Clyde Tipton."

"Really? That will prove quite helpful. Go ahead, please."

"There are five Tipton siblings. John, Clyde, Bonnie, Karen, and Cindy. While all their names are listed, their phones are not. However, under emergency contacts, Cindy's uncle John Grafton is named along with his phone and address, get this, in Phillipsburg, Saint Martin."

"That's great news."

"He is their mother's brother. That is why his last name is different. At the time of Cindy's incarceration, Bonnie and Clyde were serving their twenty-year sentences. Cindy's oldest brother, John, seems to be named after his uncle. He has protected Karen and Cindy. It is likely that Bonnie never required protection and was more aligned in age and personality with Clyde."

"We will follow-up on all of this in the morning. Tell Bucky I said hello and may the Rockets Rule."

"Their basketball team is ranked in the top twenty-five of the nation and first in the MAC conference. You are welcome to sit with me at a home game. Bucky will be in the announcer's booth through the end of the month."

"Thank you. I will take you up on that, Rosie. Bye. Have a great day. Stay safe and warm."

"I will do that. I am telling everyone that Angel ends her communication with me by telling me to stay safe. I say it is because she never felt safe in her world." Rosie's voice softened.

CHAPTER THIRTY-NINE

Angel's Recovery

Angel changed into her pajamas and nestled beneath her quilt. She propped her journal up on her knees and put her headphones on to listen to her Southern gospel music. She began to think about today, her first day back at the sewing workshop, and felt the soreness in her fingers and shoulders. This time her fingers were sore from holding a pencil and noting the completion of the masks. Another supervisor stood over the women who were sewing disposable gowns. She had a frown on her face. Angel decided to practice smiling as a form of encouragement to the inmates assigned to her.

I am so grateful to be well enough to return to work. It is true that supervision is less tiring than sitting bent over all day at the sewing machine. However, I must admit it is more rewarding to complete a flag or a mask than to praise someone who has completed hers. I need to focus on the big picture which includes developing new skills that can be important when I work outside these walls. Supervising these inmates should teach me how to interact as a boss without belittling the workers. I've never in my life overseen other workers

If I ever get out and my brothers let me work in their store, I will need to have a positive attitude, no matter how rude the customers may be. I barely hung on to minimum wage jobs. Who am I kidding? My social skills are lacking. I don't want to disappoint or embarrass them, for sure.

My boundaries are non-existent. I've been advised that I will need to develop boundaries to separate myself from the women I supervise. I can't be buddy-buddy and still expect compliance or respect. What's compliance, anyhow? I think it means doing what authority expects you to do, probably without grumbling.

I wonder how Dr. Rosie is doing, God. Please protect her and her husband and let her return to visit. It is hard to believe she can care about me when I have been such a loser in life. She must be an angel you sent to deepen my faith in you.

That's all for tonight. I love this praise music that glorifies your son, Jesus.

CHAPTER FORTY

Prostitutes or Prostituted

"Come in, Angel. How are you feeling this morning?" Dr. Jo asked.

"Much better, thanks. My headaches are still intense at times. They come and go. Weird. Not related to Covid, you know. But a little worse since then. And my fingers and back ache."

"The headaches seem to linger after Covid. But you have been prone to them, haven't you?"

"Yes, you said they are because of pinched nerves or something in my spine and neck."

"I am sorry that you can't see a specialist, Angel. Take the extra-strength Tylenol before work and then I will write you permission to take one more tablet at lunch. I wanted you to come in so I could ask you to do something for me."

"What is it, Dr. Jo? I will do anything I can. You are always so helpful to me."

"Two young women are going to join your Beautiful Life group. Chaplain Caroline and I have talked about this. They are serving time for prostitution. We are fairly certain that they were not prostituting on their own volition. In other words, they were trafficked or prostituted. They are unwilling to give up the information regarding their handlers, commonly known as pimps. They likely are too terrified to do that. And they don't trust each other not to tell the handler."

"I used to see it on the streets all the time, Dr. Jo. Girls my age or younger were forced to be prostitutes with all the money going to their pimps. Some of them were forcefully addicted to heroin, which is cheap. They have forced early abortions if they get pregnant. Very, very sad."

"We think the buyers, who are the men who pay for their services, should have equal or harsher sentences. Instead, they are charged with a misdemeanor while the girls may be charged with felonies. The laws are far too lenient."

"I have always thought that it is so unfair. Most of those men are successful, white, married men. Maybe that is why no strong penalties exist. Right?"

"Well, yes. Some law enforcement officers think it is because the buyers are congressmen, lawyers, and judges."

"So, yes, Angel, you are correct. We must help these victims by not releasing them back to their handlers. Our hands are tied if they don't admit that they are prostituting against their will. We have Christian safe homes for them. There are professionals and programs to help them overcome their brokenness and develop dignity and hope. It can begin with your group."

"The problem Dr. Jo is that what is said in the group is supposed to be confidential. If we violate their trust, they will withdraw and never again tell us how they are feeling or details about what happened to them. How do we get around that?"

"By law, Chaplain Caroline is obligated to report it if a woman feels physically threatened or if she is a threat to others. It will be anonymous and not traced back to Chappy, as you affectionately refer to her."

"Oh. I wasn't aware of that."

"It is likely that their handlers have other girls or women that are coerced into prostitution. They will be arrested when they are caught transporting those women. The arrest will not appear to be related to the women in your group."

"Okay. I get it. You are right. Sometimes a group of women live together with no means of escape. I have seen more and more women who don't even speak English, standing near hotel entrances. They cater to traveling salesmen. When I was in Juvenile Detention, I talked to a girl, about fifteen years old, who said she was escorted into a hotel by her uncle. He turned her over to three men in dark suits who were waiting to take her up an elevator with them. She was white, blonde, and American. She said her uncle had been selling her for cocaine since she was orphaned at nine. It was the saddest story, Dr. Jo."

"That is horrible. And that's the kind of young woman who ends up here if she doesn't end up dead before the age of eighteen. Dead from an overdose, abuse by her handler or buyers, or killed when she tries to escape."

"Here's another sad story. One inmate, I won't say who, said she feels like she is only worth twenty-five dollars. She has a tattoo on the back of her neck that says twenty-five dollars. This tells a potential client how much he needs to pay for her services. I saw one girl in Juvenile that had a tattoo on the inside of her bottom lip that identified her as belonging to some handler. He bailed her out and off she went to continue having sex with many men on any given evening."

"Well, Angel, it looks like you can really help us break the life sentence of some of these victims. Coming from the street, you have more knowledge than we do regarding red flags that identify these women. You might even know more than the task force made up of detectives, some of whom are operating undercover."

"I'd be glad to do that. What happens next?"

"We want you to keep your eyes and ears open in the cafeteria now that you get to go back to your meal routines. And do the same in the sewing workshop and at the chaplain's services and group meetings."

"Who do I tell when I notice or hear something said by the women?"

"If you are in the chapel or at a Bible study or group, report it to Chappy. If you are in the cafeteria, the common areas, or the sewing workshop, come and tell me. Mrs. Marigold is in direct contact with the State Highway Patrol, the local police, and the county sheriffs' offices around the state. We will collaborate with her, and she will take it from there."

"Okay."

"Good to see you are on the mend. I know you get bored when you are not working. Enjoy your new promotion and try to pace yourself through the day to conserve energy."

"Thanks, Dr. Jo."

Angel headed back to work with a new purpose in mind for the year.

CHAPTER FORTY-ONE

Sibling Love

"Here we go, Sheriff. Hopefully, Karen Tipton will know whether Uncle John has any tenants or has arranged for their housing and jobs," Amy Cunningham said.

"I doubt that she is home, Cunningham. There is no vehicle in the driveway," Sheriff Holland said.

Agent Amy Cunningham and Sheriff Thadd Holland stood on the front stoop. He opened the unlatched screen door and knocked firmly. Amy noticed the curtain on the front picture window pulled back slightly. The door opened slightly, and a woman peered around it and inquired, "what do you want?"

"Are you Karen Tipton?"

"Yes. And you are?"

"I am Sheriff Holland, and this is FBI agent Cunningham. Could we please step inside? We have a few questions to ask you about John Grafton. He is your uncle, correct?"

"Yes. I suppose you can come in, but my boyfriend, Isaac, went to the store and should be returning soon. Could you please move your car out of the driveway?"

Sheriff Holland responded in a polite voice. "Be glad to do that, Ma'am." He left Cunningham standing there while he parked in front of the house. He returned just as a late model Honda Accord pulled into the driveway. A middle-aged man wearing a Cleveland Browns baseball cap and a brown bomber jacket, quickly approached the group on the steps.

Karen Tipton explained as she let them all inside. "Isaac, these folks are asking about my Uncle John and whether he knows the whereabouts of Bonnie and Clyde."

"You've got to be kidding," Isaac said. He sat down in what appeared to be his designated chair, propped his cowboy boots up on a stool and lit a Lucky Strike.

" You can both take a seat. Want coffee or anything?"

"No thanks," they both said as they sat down on a warn, old, green couch covered with a tattered lap blanket. Karen moved Isaac's legs and sat on the stool in front of him.

"I don't have an address for Uncle John. We just e-mail each other occasionally. I haven't heard from him since before Christmas," Karen explained.

"Does he live in St. Martin year-round? Is he a resident?" Agent Cunningham said.

Cunningham had researched the St. Martin residency requirements for citizens of the United States. Both the Dutch side and the French side required that a person be gainfully employed and could produce a utility bill with an address. Otherwise, no one was legally permitted to stay more than six months.

"I don't know if he is a resident, but I do know he has a job driving a taxi. How in the world would Bonnie and Clyde have gotten to Saint Martin? Aren't they on parole or something?" Karen asked.

Changing the subject, Agent Cunningham said, "Have you seen them since they were released? Clyde was out about nine months before Bonnie." Agent Cunningham knew that Clyde had helped Karen take care of their ailing mother and John had come up to help sell her house.

"I have not seen Bonnie. I lived with our mom until she died. When Clyde got out, he came and helped, so to speak. He wasn't much help. Just lazy and more interested in his beer and marijuana. On the other hand, Uncle John helped list Mom's house and cared about how I was feeling."

"So sorry for your loss," Cunningham said.

"They know better than to come around my door. They probably don't know where I live. This is Isaac's place. Have you talked to Cindy? She is more likely to have information about them. The three of them are useless as far as I'm concerned."

Isaac piped in, "you can say that again."

"You've been very helpful, Karen. We will follow-up with Cindy. Meanwhile, if your uncle contacts you, please don't mention that we were here inquiring about Bonnie and Clyde," Sheriff Holland said.

"Okay. Hear that, Isaac? We need to help these officers find those good for nothing sibs of mine. Don't worry, we won't say a word. But don't hold your breath. My birthday isn't until June so I doubt I will hear from him soon," Karen said in a loud, huffy tone.

"Would you be willing to e-mail your Uncle John and ask how his job is going? Maybe he will share the news that they are there with him or have been, "Cunningham asked.

"Sure, I can do that."

"Then save it, along with any other communication between you, please," Cunningham added.

Cunningham and Holland stood to leave. Isaac remained seated. Sheriff Holland couldn't help but notice the long, white dog hair on the back of Agent Cunningham's trousers. He decided this wasn't the time or place to notify her. They gave Karen their cards with contact information and walked to their vehicle.

"At least we know he is a cab driver. Are you hungry? There's a Chick Filet around the corner," Cunningham said.

Holland took the opportunity to say, "yes, but I need to tell you that you have dog hair all over the back of your pants. You might want to deal with that before we enter the restaurant."

"How about we just go through the drive-thru? They are known for quick service. We can eat in the car and process what we just experienced," Cunningham said.

"Okay. Good idea. I am interested in your opinion. Weird couple, I think."

***

"That was strange, Isaac. Can you believe that Bonnie and Clyde found a way to get out of the country without passports?"

"I don't put anything past them. I would never have thought your Uncle John would harbor criminals. He seemed like a cool dude coming all the way here to help after your mother died."

"Me neither. Maybe he is hard up for cash and they promised to pay him," Karen said.

"Or maybe they just stopped there long enough to change disguises. They always were good at that. He wouldn't deny them a brief stay. He would say blood is thicker than water. Yuck."

CHAPTER FORTY-TWO

Beautiful Life

Angel arrived at the chapel twenty minutes early to set up her materials on the podium and take her usual place in the first pew on the left. There were two rows with six pews, each pew long enough to seat six people. The entire chapel was carpeted. Inmates, staff, or visitors who felt compelled to kneel as they prayed could do so comfortably.

After opening the meeting with prayer, Chaplain Caroline began by saying that she could be called Chappy or any other name not disrespectful. Several of the fourteen inmates elbowed each other and laughed. Three first time attenders just sat still and appeared self-conscious. Chappy reminded the women that everything that is said or done in the group, stays in the group, meaning that it is confidential. She asked each woman to raise her hand and state her first name or by what nickname she wanted to be called.

One of the new attendees, seated in the back row, raised her hand and announced softly that her name was Maddie. She had her arms crossed in front of her chest and made no eye contact with Chappy or anyone else. The inmate to her right patted her arm, getting her attention, and smiled. Maddie smiled back and placed her hands in her lap. Unbeknownst to the new attendees, Chappy had asked members of the group, ahead of time, to sit beside them and help them feel comfortable.

Two other attendees, seated across the aisle, also in the back of the chapel, stood together arm-in-arm. The first one, an attractive, thin, young Asian woman said that she is called Lydia. The other woman, a dark-skinned, possibly Mexican woman, with broken English, said her name is Maria. After being acknowledged by Chaplain Caroline, they quickly sat back down.

Now, standing at the podium, Angel welcomed Maddie, Lydia, and Maria by name. She recalled being seen as an unnamed piece of trash and wanted these women to have a personal identity.

Angel introduced herself and for the benefit of the new women, explained that she is from Toledo, is a lifer, and has been incarcerated for twenty-six years. Her voice was strong and clear. She then explained she wanted to share a story from the Bible and there would be a discussion on how each of them can relate to the Samaritan woman. She chose not to read the story of Jesus with the Samaritan woman at the well, but to tell it. Angel thought that telling it would evoke more emotion. When she first heard it, she felt a slight tinge of hope. When she finished speaking, Chaplain Caroline passed out copies of the story as found in the Bible, Book of John, Chapter Four. She included four questions at the end.

The first question: Do you believe that God loves you?

The second question: If so, why and if not, why not?

The third question: Do you believe God has the power to rescue you?

The fourth question: Do you pray and if so, do you believe God hears your prayers? If not, why not?

"How many of you believe that God loves you? That He loves you unconditionally?" Angel asked.

Of the fourteen group members, nine smiled at Angel, and raised their hands. Two looked at Angel with slumped shoulders and tears in their eyes. Of the three new women, all simply hung their heads.

Angel quietly explained, "It was extremely difficult for me to believe that God could love me after everything I had done or was involved in that violated his commandments. Chappy and this group helped me to see that God is a loving God whose love for me is not based on my behavior but because I am his child. If like me, you have not had the unconditional love of an earthly father, or even mother, you can't begin to understand what real love is about. God doesn't walk away from us. We walk away from him. He is waiting for your return, my sisters. And he knows you by name."

Everyone was speechless. Finally, the silence was broken by one of the five who seemed to doubt God's love. She was not new. She was sitting in the first row on the aisle. She said, "My name is Kitty. So,

Angel, how do I prove to God that I won't do that stuff anymore when I am in prison? Why would he believe me?"

Angel stood beside Kitty and asked, "Who would like to answer that question?"

A dark-skinned woman with flecks of gray hair, seated directly behind Kitty raised her hand, remained seated, and began to speak.

"Hi. My name is Char. I would like to answer that."

Kitty turned around to face Char. Angel acknowledged Char who was a regular attendee of the group, and said, "Please do."

"If you start reading the Bible, Kitty, you will see that God doesn't expect us to be perfect. He knows your heart. If you are sincere about changing when you are released, he will accept that promise from you. He always keeps his promises to love us," Char said with a warm smile.

A few women said Amen out loud.

"Thank you, Char," Angel said. "You explained that so beautifully. Don't you agree sisters?"

Most of the women nodded in agreement. They saw the group as a sisterhood of believers. The doubting members just stared at Angel. However, the three new members seemed to listen intently.

"How about God's power and the power of prayer?" Angel asked.

"What can I pray about when I know how long my sentence will be? He won't interfere with that right? Plus, I prayed not to be arrested and look where it got me," Betty Jean, one of the doubting group members suddenly shouted out.

"Let me answer that, Betty Jean. God has a purpose for your life. We have talked about that. It took me a lot of years here, filled with self-imposed hardship, to realize that and to find my purpose. In terms of being arrested, I finally realized that if I was still on the street, well I wouldn't be, because it is likely I would be dead."

"How do I find that purpose?" Betty Jean asked.

"By spending time every day in the Word, as the Bible is known, and praying. I pray gratitude and find something to give thanks for even if it is that I survived this day. And by quieting yourself to listen. And by believing the Holy Spirit lives in your heart," Angel said.

Chaplain Caroline added, "Believing in God doesn't mean you won't face problems and challenges, Betty Jean. It means you trust that he will be with you through it all. Read the Book of Ruth and see how he directed her journey after terrible, tragic hardships."

Again, a few Amens could be heard.

"Let's take some prayer requests and then share some praises or gratitude you feel. State your first name so we can jot down who you are and what you need. Angel and I encourage you to pray for one another each evening. If you need a pencil, raise your hand and Angel will bring you one," Chappy said.

Prayer requests included prayers for forgiveness, prayers for their children, prayers for patience with other inmates, and prayers for strength to cope with their circumstances.

Praises ranged from receiving e-mails from loved ones, money in their commissary accounts, quarantine ending, and overcoming Covid.

"Angel, thank you for co-leading the group today. Maddie, Lydia, and Maria, we welcome you to our group Beautiful Life. See you next week. Be kind to one another."

The women filed out of the chapel. Angel wondered what the stories of the new members entailed. They were all serving time on charges of prostitution, drug possession with intent to distribute, and receiving stolen property. Who were their handlers? Did they know one another or live together? Were they addicted? What property did they receive? From whom?"

Angel went directly to Mrs. Marigold's office. She needed her questions answered so she could privately address the issues with each of the three women. Of course, she would need to earn their trust before she could expect them to open up to her. Co-leading the group was one step in that direction.

CHAPTER FORTY-THREE

Trafficked

"Angel. I am so glad you stopped in," Mrs. Marigold said.

"I have a couple of questions to ask you," Angel said.

"Please come in and sit down," Mrs. Marigold said as she came around her desk.

"Thank you. I was wondering if you can give me some information on the three new women in our Beautiful Life Group?"

"Tell me their names. What exactly do you need?"

"Two of them, Lydia and Maria, sat together. I think they may have been arrested together. Lydia is Asian and Maria is Hispanic, possibly Mexican. Then Maddie was by herself and Caucasian. Can you tell me what their charges are and if any of them were addicted?"

"Yes. You are correct in assuming that Lydia and Maria were together. And, yes, they spent ten days in the infirmary for detox. Their sentences would have been reduced if they had given the police detectives the names of their handlers and dealers. They would not. The handlers were their "pimps," and their dealers were likely part of an international, organized crime group.

The women are clean but still terrified. If they disclose information, the traffickers told them that their families will pay the price. Both were transported here with the threat that if they refused to come to the USA, their younger siblings would be snatched."

"If I get that information and pass it on, won't they and their families be in danger? Where are the girls from?"

"Lydia is from Manilla in the Philippines. She is known as a Filipino. Lydia and her younger brother, Gabriel, were brought here under the guise of schooling and employment opportunities. Her parents were very poor, and they were told that Lydia could be a model in the United States. She was sold to the Chinese mob and transported to Ohio instead of Hollywood.

They were also told that their son, Gabriel, could be a gardener and "pool boy" for a wealthy Los Angeles family who owned three prestigious restaurants near Hollywood. He could go to school and study to become a chef in one of their restaurants. None of which was true.

Lydia's brother was rescued from what is commonly known as domestic servitude when the restaurant was busted for selling cocaine. He was discovered in a closet where the restaurant owners locked him up during the restaurant's hours of operation. At night he cleaned floors and prepped vegetables for soup and stir fry dishes to be offered to customers the next day. He received no pay and was told that he was paying back the cost of his and his sister's transportation.

Maria is from Acapulco, Mexico. Her parents owned a hotel and she disappeared from school one day. She was fourteen. She wasn't expected back at the hotel until 6:00 p.m. By then, she had been snatched for ten hours. They believe she planned to meet a sixteen-year-old boy at an ice cream store. When her e-mails were checked, it turned out that the person was a forty-year-old man, posing as a sixteen-year-old boy. They believe she was groomed to be snatched."

"Mrs. Marigold, what is groomed?"

"That is when a relationship between the child and perpetrator is formed over time to build trust and to get the minor to agree to meet in person. Often the grooming takes place on-line."

"That's terrible. I thought I was street wise. I never heard about any of this stuff. Now, I am worried that it would be obvious to the bad people that the arrests or busts resulted from Lydia or Maria providing information?"

"With so many women, girls, and boys, arrested every day, the organizations will be hard pressed to single out the two of them. When the girls complete their sentences, they will be released to their handlers. Surveillance and a stake-out will begin immediately. Someone undercover will purchase them for a party to be hosted by the prominent mayor of a nearby, large city. They likely will be just two of a dozen young women delivered to the party. When the buyers, prominent men, and corrupt local officials, get busted along with the handlers, Lydia and Maria shouldn't be suspected.

As far as Maddie's story goes, she was a victim of familial trafficking. Her mother sold her for drugs from the age of nine. They were known as trailer trash. They lived in a run-down trailer with no indoor plumbing . When she was fifteen, Children's Protective Services picked her up as she left an abortion clinic and approached a car parked at the curb. They had been alerted by several pro-life women who volunteered across the street at a Christian pregnancy center."

"Was she arrested?"

"No, she had broken no laws. The abortion clinic was shut down and the doctors arrested for performing an abortion without the consent of a parent or guardian. Maddie said it was her third abortion."

"What happened next?"

"She was placed in a foster family. She felt such shame, she began cutting herself and ended up in the emergency room. She walked out of the hospital without being released. She wasn't seen again by authorities until she was arrested for soliciting men on Superbowl Sunday last year. It is the biggest day of the year for prostitution and trafficking of minors."

"How did she get sentenced here?"

"She was released to her handler, and he beat her up severely for being arrested and costing him money. She resorted to shoplifting to get arrested and thereby protecting her from him. She is here for her safety and because she is the link to breaking up that particular syndicate and rescuing their trafficked girls. No one can know that, Angel."

"I won't tell anybody. Can I approach her and become her friend?"

"Let me get back to you about that. Meanwhile, I have good news for you. Your brothers, Greg and Mike Kessler, called to get permission to visit you. Can you fill out the request forms to allow them to visit?" Mrs. Marigold handed Angel the forms and a pen.

"Are you kidding? Of course, I'll fill them out. Oh, my gosh. I wonder what they will look like as middle-aged men. They were practically babies when I ran away."

"Barring any snowstorms or Covid outbreaks, they will be here next Saturday. Don't worry. Even if they are sewing, you will be released from work. I will see to it that they have a debit card so you can have drinks and snacks. Congratulations, Angel. You deserve this reconciliation."

CHAPTER FORTY-FOUR

The Kessler Brothers

Greg and Mike signed the visitor's log at the visitation auditorium. The officer directed them to a table in front of the room near the stage. They no sooner sat down than their sister, Angel, appeared in the doorway. She looked far different than she did twenty-six years ago, on the day of her sentencing hearing. Back then, she had long, straggly hair, weighed about twenty pounds more, and seemed taller. As she approached them, they stood. Today in her orange jumpsuit, she walked with her shoulders slumped. As she approached them, they stood and smiled to conceal their true feeling of shame for not staying in touch. They were advised by the visitation officer, not to hug or touch the inmate, partially because it was a rule and more importantly, so they didn't spread Covid.

"Oh my gosh. Look at you two. You are both so handsome. I can't believe you have come all this way to see me. I love you so much," Angel said.

"We were happy to hear from Dr. Rosie Klein and to know where you are and that we can come and visit," Greg said.

"We talk about you and pray for you, Angel. How are you?" Mike asked.

"I'm doing good. We were locked down because of Covid and I had kind of a bad case of it. But I'm okay now. How about you guys?"

"We have a coffee shop and ice cream store located in a lodge that our parents manage. It is in Petosky Michigan. Have you heard of Petosky? It is an expensive, well-known town for tourists who love to ski," Mike said.

"No. I am an Ohio girl, remember? My grandma thought you were in Michigan. My dream is to have my sentence commuted and be allowed to leave the state. Then I can visit you and meet your families. Mike, you have kids, right?"

"I have two sons and a stepdaughter. I married a sweet Christian woman, Rachel, that I met through a church retreat held at Evergreen lodge. She was divorced so when I married her it was a package deal. I bought an engagement ring for her five-year-old daughter, Cloe. Our first child together is due in mid-summer. Don't know if we are having a boy or girl," Mike said.

"Our parents, the Kessler's, used to work in the summer at a Christian Camp near Jackson Michigan. My wife, Shannon, was a camp counselor for ten-year-old girls, and I was in charge of the horse barn. When we were about twenty, Shannon married a guy she met in college. Her husband was not a Christian. When a believer marries a non-believer, it is called unevenly yoked. They divorced after graduation, and she returned to the camp to work summers in the dining hall. We resumed our friendship and it blossomed into more. We married at the camp the following summer," Greg said.

"You and Shannon have kids?"

"Yes. They are four and five, Erik and Todd. You probably remember taking care of us at that age," Greg said.

"I do. You guys were a handful. But we loved each other, didn't we?" Angel asked.

"You had your hands full, Angel. I remember being at a store when you stole some food. The manager caught you. He felt sorry for us and gave us even more food to take home. He meant well. But as I look back, I wonder how our lives would have been different if he had reported us to Children's Services. Greg's and my life ended up great, but your life was filled with misery," Mike said.

"I never thought of that, Mike," Angel said.

"It sounds neat. How are your parents?"

"They are fine. They are busy managing Evergreen lodge that sits down the road from our houses. We each live on five acres with a woods and a creek separating our properties. Dad is not preaching anymore but Mom plays the piano at our church," Greg answered. "The four of us sing in a quartet, mostly southern gospel but some contemporary music too."

"We aren't here to talk about us. We're here to listen to how you are doing and how you spend your time," Mike said.

" We sew flags. Before Covid, I used to sew the side hems and the bottom hems. During the height of Covid we sewed two million masks and twenty-thousand disposable gowns. We mostly are back to sewing Ohio flags and some flags representing Ohio colleges. I am a supervisor now."

"That keeps you busy, doesn't it? Greg asked.

"It does. Makes the days pass quickly. Then I also help our chaplain run groups so the women can adjust to being locked up and to develop a relationship with God," Angel said.

"You're a Christian, then?" Mike asked.

"I am baptized," Angel said. "A local church brings these huge metal tubs to the courtyard every three months. Women who believe in Jesus and ask for forgiveness of their sins can request to be baptized."

"That's amazing, Angel."

Angel felt pleased that she gained her brothers' approval at last. She used to be sad when she thought about how disappointed they must be in her. First, because she ran away, leaving them by themselves, little boys in their abusive environment. Secondly, she lived a life of crime that they could never have understood.

"The best time of my life in Ohio was when we went to the little church a few blocks away on Wednesday nights. We had supper that I didn't have to fix you. We played games and we sang hymns. It was so much fun. And for a few hours we could forget about what we were going home to," Angel said. "I felt close to Jesus, and I wanted to have that feeling again."

"You know that when you get out of here, you are welcome to come to Petosky and live with one of us. You can rotate houses if you want," Both brothers laughed.

"Shannon and Rachel will love you, Angel. You can babysit the boys and they will get to know their Auntie Angel," Greg said.

"That would be a dream come true.

"You can work in the store, or our parents would give you a job in the lodge."

"You can babysit so Shannon and I can have a date night now and then." Greg said.

"Double-date, Greg?" Mike asked.

"No. I don't want to hurt your feelings bro, but we need a romantic dinner with candlelight and no spilt milk," Greg said. Mike laughed.

"Spilt milk?" Angel asked.

"The little guys find a way to interrupt us when we attempt to eat dinner, and don't pay attention to them. Sometimes they resort to messing up the table or floor with spilt milk and think it is funny," Greg looked at his brother and laughed.

"I'm curious. Where is Amanda? Is she okay?" Angel asked.

"She and her husband just came up and spent Christmas with us. Their twin daughters, Emily and Eva, came too. They are adults, of course, but still single," Mike said.

"Wow. Let me get this straight, I am an aunt of six kids who will likely adore me." They laughed.

"This has been wonderful. I hope we can stay connected. Please call us collect, any time," Greg said.

"I can't thank you both, enough. Stay safe and I will be praying for your families. Oh, and you can write to me and keep me updated on your families."

"Great idea, Angel. "We will do that for sure," Mike responded.

The brothers glanced toward the visitation officer's station by the door. The three of them quickly engaged in a group hug. Tears clouded their eyes. The brothers swallowed hard to enable themselves to say I love you to their big sister.

Then Greg and Mike stayed positioned. As Angel was led out of the room by Officer Mitchell, she turned to look at them one more time. In turn, they both waved. The brothers signed out and silently walked back to the visitor's parking lot.

CHAPTER FORTY-FIVE

Deportation

At two-thirty in the afternoon, Bonnie and Clyde's uncle, John Grafton, Bonnnie and Clyde's uncle, parked his bumble bee yellow taxi in the waiting area across the narrow, side road from the Princess Juliana International Airport. There were twenty or more plane spotters, the nickname for those who parked there, along with the local patrons of an outdoor bar, watching the spectacular landings and take-offs. They enjoyed seeing the jets arrive from and depart to France, The Netherlands, and the U.S.A.

John had responded to a call from the dispatcher of his company saying that three Americans were scheduled to arrive at two o'clock on Delta Airlines. They requested transportation to the Saphire Beach Hotel and said they were referred to a driver by the name of Big John. The dispatcher couldn't help but laugh out loud since the name was completely descriptive of John.

As usual, John expected them to take forty-five minutes to come through customs and retrieve their luggage. He released his seat belt, leaned his seat back, pushed his ball cap with the taxi company logo down over his eyes, and took a brief "power" nap.

Meanwhile, Agent Liza Cunningham, Sheriff Thadd Holland, and Agent Ron Thompson walked across the tarmac to the small frame building where they would be asked to produce their passports and explain to the customs agent that they would be on the island for a week. They stated their purpose was to tour the island, enjoy their time-share and experience other tourist attractions. Actually, they were searching for Bonnie and Clyde Tipton, fugitives from the law. They proceeded to the luggage carousel and grabbed their suitcases. It appeared that they were intact and had not been searched. They brought no detectable weapons, but Agent Cunningham was permitted to bring mace as an acceptable means of self-protection for women tourists or residents.

John drove up to the curb and couldn't help but notice the two well-built, middle-aged men and a younger, attractive, female companion wearing Notre Dame ball caps. He exited his taxi and introduced himself as their designated driver. They acknowledged him and confirmed their destination. John opened the trunk, put their luggage inside, and came around to open the door for Cunningham. She sat beside him while the two male Notre Dame fans sat in the back seat. John, tipped graciously by Agent Thompson, was instructed to pick them up in the morning and take them for a tour and then to his favorite beach. A time was agreed upon.

The three "tourists" checked into the Saphire Beach Hotel located on the Dutch side of the island. A tall, blonde haired, young bellhop led them to a two-story villa, located beyond the swimming pool, directly above the Caribbean Sea. This time Sheriff Holland tipped the young man and thanked him warmly.

Sheriff Holland and Agent Thompson stepped out onto their balcony that included a small, private hot tub, and immediately stretched out on two chaise lounges, leaving a third lounge empty between them. While they admired the view, Agent Cunningham quickly selected the master bedroom suite for herself, checked out the small refrigerator sitting against the wall in the corner of the living area, and grabbed three bottles of pre-mixed Margaritas. She put three tall glasses into an ice bucket and approached the men with the drinks. She was not surprised to find them sound asleep with their shoes removed and their hats down over their eyes. She decided to recline between them, remove her shoes, breathe the fresh air, and enjoy her Margarita on the rocks.

Later, over dinner at the pool bar, they planned their disguises and approaches for the next day. At 10:00 a.m., John pulled up in front of the hotel. This time, Sheriff Holland jumped into the front seat. Agent Cunningham took her camera out of her beach bag and sat behind Big John. Agent Thompson leaned forward and made small talk with the two in the front seat.

"So where are we heading?" Holland asked.

"I thought you might want to go up into the hills so you could take pictures of the cruise ships in the harbor of Philipsburg and the spectacular view of the harbor. Then we can head toward the beach where you can relax and have lunch served. You don't want to shop on the days that the ships dock because the stores and outdoor merchants up their prices. Later in the week, you can barter for items made by locals like hand-woven purses and baskets."

"Okay John," Cunningham said. "Nothing better than getting things at bargain prices."

The men laughed. The taxi began its journey up a winding, narrow road with small, thatched roof houses on either side and dogs stretched out in front of wide-open doorways.

The three had planned to use the day just to stake out Bonnie and Clyde and then make contact with local authorities to get their cooperation in extraditing these fugitives.

Agent Thompson had put out a written Red Notice to the Chief Commissioner of the Saint Martin police force, which was part of the Interpol National Central Bureau (NCB). It identified Bonnie and Clyde Tipton as fugitives from the U.S.A. Their names, nationalities, descriptions of hair color and eye color, birthdates, photos, and fingerprints were forwarded to all Interpol member countries. This was a formal request for assistance with fighting international crime and safeguarding the nation's borders.

One assistant commissioner oversaw the uniformed police officers on the island, while a second assistant commissioner, Commissioner Hale, was over all national and international criminal investigations. Commissioner Hale responded affirmatively to their request for identification, arrest, and deportation to the United States for trial and sentencing. He was extremely interested and concerned for the safety of his citizens when he heard they had served time for the sex trafficking of minors.

"Well, folks, I'll take you to Baie Rouge, the most beautiful beach on the French side of the Island, with the most magnificent, flavorful, grilled ribs to be found anywhere."

"Sounds great," Cunningham said.

"I can come back at 4:00 p.m. if you like. The couple I am picking up at the airport will arrive at 2:00 p.m. just as you folks did yesterday. Once they are delivered to their Bed and Breakfast, I can return them for you. That will work, won't it?"

Little did Big John know that his services would not be required for transportation. The local authorities are on standby. They are waiting for Bonnie and Clyde to be positively identified. Agent Thompson is assigned to notify them as to the specific location on the beach. Thompson was told they will remain in the local prison until arrangements are made for their transportation.

"Big John will be arrested for harboring fugitives. He will be deported, his property confiscated, and authorities will be waiting for him when he disembarks in the United States. There he will be charged with harboring fugitives and obstruction of justice," Thompson explained to Cunningham and Holland.

Big John parked the taxi. Agent Cunningham took her sunglasses and floppy straw hat out of her beach bag. She pulled her hat down over her face and stepped out of the car. Thompson and Holland were wearing ball caps with a Cancun logo, tee shirts, and cargo shorts. Big John led them down a trail to the white, sand beach directly in front of where the Tipton's were preparing ribs. Positioned twenty yards closer to the water were colorful, pastel Adirondack chairs with wide arms. Food and drink could be placed on them. They sat down. Big John told them to relax, eat lunch, and enjoy their afternoon. He headed back toward the parking area. He waved at Bonnie and Clyde who acknowledged him by returning the same friendly gesture.

Cunningham took a book out of her beach bag and began to read. The men stretched their legs out, pulled the brims of their hats over their eyes, placed their arms across their chests, and appeared to take a nap.

Forty-five minutes later, all three of them approached the Tipton's. They ordered ribs with grilled veggies from Bonnie. Clyde kept his head down and continued cooking. He was slender with a grey ponytail, a red kerchief tied around his forehead, and a solid, black tank top.

"You might want to sit at a table under an umbrella," Bonnie suggested to them. "It is more comfortable to have a bit of shade when you eat. I'll bring your food when it's ready."

"Good idea," Cunningham said as she headed for a nearby table. It occurred to her that Bonnie was either wearing a wig or had dyed her hair black, and that she had blue contact lenses.

The men followed carrying three bottles of Caribe, the most popular beer among locals on the French side of the Island. At the poolside bar of their hotel, they were told that Corona is the favorite at Dutch establishments.

When they sat down, Holland picked up the large plastic bottle of barbecue sauce and read the label. "Can you believe it? Montgomery Inn Barbecue Sauce from Cincinnati Ohio served all the way down here. I thought it would be something made in the Caribbean area."

"No way. You've got to be kidding," Cunningham said. "I doubt that it was transported by the current proprietors. They don't want to be identified as Ohioans, that's for sure."

Just then, Bonnie brought their lunches on a small round tray. Grilled vegetables and barbecued ribs along with tall, narrow shot glasses of Tequila. Complimentary they were told.

"Thanks. What is your name?" Thompson asked.

"My name is Lola," Bonnie answered quickly. She was clearly not accustomed to that question. Most tourists didn't care about her name, only that she served them complimentary liquor.

"Well. You and your partner do a nice job. How long have you had this food stand?" Thompson asked as he slipped her a ten-dollar tip.

She lied and said, "We've been here three winter seasons. In the summer we travel to Ontario where it is cooler."

"Oh, so you're Canadian. How did you find this Island and this opportunity?" Holland asked.

"We read about it in a Windsor paper. The previous owner didn't want to just walk away so he advertised this little business, and we thought what the heck. And here we are."

"How neat. Glad it worked out for you." Cunningham said.

"Let me know if you need another beer, tequila, or anything." Bonnie turned her back and quickly walked away.

"Lola from Windsor. That was quick thinking on her part, don't you think?" Cunningham asked.

"Oh, I don't know. It was probably well rehearsed but just not often used. Wonder what she would have named her brother?" Holland laughed.

After finishing their lunches and using bottled water to wipe off their sticky fingers, they returned to their chairs and pretended to relax.

It wasn't long before two burly men and a petite young woman in uniform came barreling on foot, weapons drawn, down the hill from the parking area. They advanced on Bonnie and Clyde from behind and soon had them cuffed with their backs to the officers. They announced that they were local police officers, and they were both under arrest. The woman frisked Bonnie and one of the men frisked Clyde. They led them up to the parking area where two police cars were parked with a driver seated in each. Bonnie was placed in the back seat with the lady officer. In the other patrol car, Clyde was seated between the two arresting officers. The duo had no time to concoct a story as to why they are innocent of all charges in the U.S.A.

So as not to blow their cover, Cunningham, Holland, and Thompson acted surprised at the arrests. They remained on the beach in their chairs to see whether the Tipton's were part of a crime group. No one approached the food stand or walked on the beach with any interest. Holland called the taxi company and cancelled their pick-up by Big John. He was arrested at the airport waiting area prior to the arrival of his next fare. Sound asleep.

"That was exciting, wasn't it?" Cunningham asked.

"I guess. I heard this morning from Commissioner Hale, that to speed up the process, they would be deported instead of extradited to the United States. Extradition is more expensive and might be difficult to justify, since their crime is breaking parole and whatever the charge is for poisoning Dr. Klein's dog. Those do not measure up to extradition standards. But the Chief Commissioner wants them off his Island immediately. They fear for the safety of children and women. They know they already served their time for those sex trafficking offenses and worry they might start it up again." Thompson explained.

"They don't expect us to take them back, do they?" Holland asked.

"No. Other arrangements have been made. Our flights home are tomorrow and our police escort back to the hotel is standing up there on the hill. So much for a leisurely day at the beach. How about we grab a chaise lounge at the Blue Saphire pool and enjoy a refreshing Margarita on the rocks?" Cunningham asked.

"Sounds like a great plan. At least with the police driving us back there, a tip won't be required. We can save that for the pool bartender." They all laughed.

CHAPTER FORTY-SIX

Angel's Intervention

"Good morning, Angel," Chaplain Caroline said as Angel tapped on her half-opened office door.

"Good morning, Chappy" Angel said. "You sent a message to the sewing workshop for me to come down to your office?"

"Yes, I have been praying for the three young ladies who attended our Beautiful Life group and thinking about how you can serve as a strong encouragement to them. How about if we invite them to a small group session with just the three of them and the two of us?"

"That sounds like a great idea. I know when I first started attending, I felt too guilty and too self-conscious to say anything personal in a group setting. I wouldn't have admitted all that I had done even to you, let alone other inmates."

"I remember, Angel. You were so broken, damaged in so many ways. I am very proud of you and of how your testimony has rescued women from the private hell they experience and their feelings of being all alone."

"Thank you. How should we go about this plan?"

"Let's invite them to this private office for tea on Saturday afternoon. The small, round table will be conducive for talking. I will open with prayer. Then I will give them Women's Devotional Bibles and small, leather journals and pens. Why don't you explain how you use your journals to record your feelings and thoughts as well as prayers? Then tell them how you ended up in prison, concluding with how life has changed knowing that God is by your side."

"That's a good idea. I will hold off sharing my entire life's story and will just let them hear what led to me being sentenced to life."

"That should create some conversation. At the very least, you can ask them if they have any questions. Finally, I will ask each one of them how they happened to be sent here. We will see how open they become and not push them to disclose anything uncomfortable."

"It sounds like a great idea, Chappy."

"I will let you know when the plan is completed, Angel. Thank you for coming to the office."

"No, thank you Chappy for including me in the small group. "They both stood and hugged each other. Angel put her head briefly on Chaplain Caroline's shoulder.

CHAPTER FORTY-SEVEN

Tapestry Group

Dr. Jo was setting up the chairs in a circle for the Friday evening Tapestry Group meeting. Angel walked into the room and put her notebook on a seat to hold her place. She walked over to the table where complimentary decaf, ice water, and warm chocolate chip cookies were available.

"Hi, Angel. Welcome. Glad to see you are well from that nasty virus that was going around. Quarantine is no fun, is it?"

"I am feeling much better. Stronger. I have never in my life felt as weak. Quarantine is only bad when you are better and antsy to walk around. I didn't notice it for about two weeks. How many are you expecting tonight, Dr. Jo?" Angel asked. She sat back down, placed her cookie on her notebook in her lap and her cup of hot, black coffee on the carpet beside her chair.

"If everyone shows up, we should have twelve. That is not to say that they will have completed their homework. I have materials you can hand out to the women joining us for the first time. Three new women were invited. You look prepared. I see you brought your notebook."

"I had time to work hard on the thought stopping technique for "stinkin thinkin" you taught us. Being sick leaves a lot of time to think. That is when you aren't sleeping."

"You are right about that. I can't wait to hear how it worked for you. Here come a few of the ladies. It appears there are a couple of women I don't recognize," Dr. Jo said.

Angel turned around and was surprised to see Maddie and Maria entering the room. No sign of Lydia. She thought if Maria attended certainly Lydia would too. Her eyes caught their attention and she waved and smiled at them. They sat down in the two seats to Angel's left. Maddie was beside her. Her odor permeated the air. It brought back a childhood memory of Angel's. She recalled deliberately wetting herself to attempt to avoid Rossi's attempt to molest her. Could it be, she wondered, that Maddie was accustomed to using the same tactic and had not yet felt safe enough to take showers? Or was the habit so ingrained that it didn't occur to her to get clean? At that moment, Maria moved to the other side of Angel. Was it to be friendly or to avoid the smell?

Dr. Jo began the group session by inviting the women to help themselves to a beverage and a cookie. She asked each woman to say her name and the reason she wants to change their thinking or problem solving. She began with Angel.

"My name is Angel. I have "stinkin thinkin" when I am tired, discouraged, sick, or even bored. I have learned from Dr. Jo that what you think about yourself, your past, or your circumstances will create your beliefs. Now, I have learned to change my thoughts and my attitude has changed for the better most of the time. I am not perfect. At times I fall back into old habits."

"Thank you, Angel. Later you can share your new techniques for stopping negative, self-defeating thoughts," Dr. Jo said.

"I am Maria. I know I need help with how I think about my future. I was from Mexico and don't speak English well. I was as you say, trafficked to the United States. I was arrested for prostitution. I was bailed out and beaten badly. Then I resorted to shoplifting to get arrested again. I have only been here in prison a week and I feel very helpless and scared. I do feel safer in here than I have felt on the outside for a long time." Maria put her head down and wiped away a tear.

Angel placed her hand over Maria's hand and gave it a little squeeze.

"Thank you for coming, Maria. All the women here have experienced the same feelings and thoughts as you."

In turn, the other women told their names and said what caused them to join the group. When it came to the last woman, Maddie, she very softly stated her name and remained speechless for a moment. She took a deep breath and said, "I have never been invited to anything and for the first time, I felt like someone actually noticed me. Thank you, Dr. Jo."

"You are very welcome, Maddie. Welcome to Tapestry. Angel, would you please share how you have succeeded, usually, in changing your thinking habits?"

"When a negative thought comes into my mind, I find a way to distract myself. I might pick up a book to read or draw or listen to music. The idea is to look at or listen to or do something to stop your thoughts. But being human, as Dr. Jo would say, the thoughts about myself or my situation in life creep back into my mind. Then, I gently slap my cheek and say to myself if I am in a crowd, "Stop It." If I am alone, I say it out loud. When it happens a third time, I slap harder and say, "Stop it. I mean it." If I need to, I grab my journal and write my thoughts down with the corrected ones. That's it. It takes practice."

"Let's open it up for questions. Does anyone want to ask Angel anything?"

"Surprisingly, Maria raised her hand. "When what you are thinking about yourself is true, how do you change your thinking?"

"To begin with, Maria, if you are thinking you are worthless, you are wrong. God made you and he doesn't make no trash."

With that, Maddie's head popped up. Angel reminded herself that she was told that Maddie was called "white trash".

"So, whatever label you are putting on yourself, you need to change it to think that God is a good God and has a good future planned for you."

Other women asked Angel questions and shared what they had written in their journals about how they were stopping their negative thinking and feeling hopeful about their futures.

The group was dismissed by Dr. Jo. Angel walked out of the office beside Maddie, who was avoided by the others, not for who she is but for how she smelled. Angel knew that Dr. Jo would approach her about her hygiene and for now, she needed the unconditional support of a friend.

CHAPTER FORTY-EIGHT

Courses Approved

Verna Mitchell stood over Angel as she napped with her arms were bent over her eyes to shield them from the light. Her journal was spread open across her chest. "Angel, you have a couple visitors this afternoon. I will take you down to the professional visitation room," Officer Mitchell said.

Angel wiped her eyes, closed her journal, placed it under her pillow, stretched her arms upward, and then sat on the edge of her bed to put on her shoes. Who could be here, she wondered?

"Really? Let me put my shoes on and brush my hair and teeth," Angel said.

As Angel approached the visitation room with its glass windows, metal door with windows beginning midway up, she recognized her attorneys, Travis and Devon Gump. They were sitting beside one another at a table in the center of the room. She wondered what prompted them to visit her, unannounced, on a cold, snowy Saturday. They stood and smiled.

Once Angel and her visitors were seated, Officer Mitchell left the room and locked the door. No need to remain positioned there since she saw no threat of violence to any of them. She proceeded down the hall to the officer's break room.

"Good afternoon, Angel. How are you?" Travis asked.

"I'm okay. My back and joints ache, but aside from that, I'm doing fine. Back to work after Covid."

"We have some good news to share. There is an international service sorority with chapters in Toledo and Dayton. They raise money for worthy causes and non-profit organizations. Dr. Klein had occasion to speak at one of their luncheon meetings. She, of course, mentioned you and your thirst for knowledge. Dr. Klein told them there are no books in the prison library that offer information that interests you.

You've been incarcerated so long; you have read everything that you found interesting."

"That was very nice of Dr. Klein. Wow. And it is very true. The books have all been donated and no information is coming in on the subjects I like to read about."

"The Toledo chapter voted to pay for a couple of Great Courses. The courses are online and usually involve twenty-four, thirty-minute classes on a given topic. The sorority wanted to know what you would enjoy learning," Devon said.

"Dr. Klein told them that you have a servant's heart and like to help inmates. She contacted Chaplain Wexler who told her that there are quite a few deaf inmates who have extreme difficulty communicating with the officers, staff, and other women. Dr. Klein recalled evaluating a deaf person for competency to stand trial. She had two ASL interpreters in the room with her. It was extremely time-consuming and took a lot of patience on the part of the deaf defendant and Dr. Klein," Travis said.

"Would you like to learn American Sign Language known as ASL to help those deaf inmates?" Devon asked.

"I would love to do that. The deaf girls shut down and we don't know how to communicate with them, and they don't even try to communicate with us. They live in their own little world, reading lips, and using their hands to talk to each other."

"The second course that was recommended by Dr. Jo, is cooking. Again, it entails twenty-four, thirty-minute lessons. She said you are interested in nutrition and healthy lifestyles."

"Oh, my gosh. That's awesome. If I ever get released, I will likely work in some form of food service. My brothers have a coffee and ice cream shop in a lodge in Petosky Michigan. They have said I could work for them. Maybe I could add daily soups and salads to their menu."

"Chaplain Wexler, I guess you call her Chappy, has agreed to have you come to her office on Sunday afternoons and take the courses on-line. You can both watch. She will take the ASL classes with you. Then you can be practice partners," Travis said.

"This is a dream come true. I don't know how I can ever thank you guys, Chappy, and Dr. Rosie," Angel said with her voice wavering with emotion.

Travis and Devon stood, and Angel followed suit. Officer Mitchell placed her coffee on a ledge across the hall and opened the door.

"Goodbye, Angel. We will be back in touch. Glad you are interested in these courses," Travis said.

"Officer Mitchell, did you hear the exciting news? I get to take American Sign Language and cooking classes on-line."

"No, Angel. The professional visitation rooms are soundproof and there are no microphones recording your conversations. Besides that, I don't read lips," Verna Mitchell laughed.

"That is so great, Angel. I know you will enjoy doing that." Officer Mitchell said.

The Gump's left the restricted area, turned in their visitor badges, and retrieved their photo IDs. They smiled at one another as they walked out to the car.

CHAPTER FORTY-NINE

Rosie's Farewell

"Hi Bucky. I am safely settled at Daisy Marigold's house. How has your day been?"

"My day went well. I was working from home so you can guess where Willow spent this afternoon."

"Depending on where you spent it, I imagine. Did the two of you take involuntary naps?"

"You know us too well, Rosie. What is your plan for tomorrow?"

"I will have a light breakfast here with Daisy and then go spend time with Angel. She has new skills she wants to share with me. I only wish that she could have been granted a parole hearing. She so much wants to be heard. But on a positive note, I heard from the warden that when she has served thirty, it is more likely to be approved."

"You did the best you could, Rosie. And you had quite a team outside the prison walls and inside as well."

"I am grateful that the Gump's and I were able to enlist the service sorority's support to donate the courses for her. And I am grateful that she has Daisy Marigold, Officer Mitchell, Dr. Jo, and Chaplain Caroline in her corner. They make up a great team of caring professionals."

"Enjoy your time with her and let me know when you are back on the road. What time is your reunion tomorrow night?"

"It's at six-thirty. It's just dinner and time to chat with classmates. I guess there is a little entertainment. I am sorry it is limited to classmates only."

"Don't be. I have a meeting with Sean Simmons. Remember him? Captain of my University baseball team and then Baseball coach after I was promoted to Athletic Director."

"Of course."

"He is on the short list for Athletic Director. It means my complete retirement will become a reality very soon, possibly before June ends."

"Sounds like an extended vacation could be in the making. Maybe we can stay in Austria when our volunteer work is completed at Haus Edelweiss." Rosie laughed.

"Love you. See you on Sunday afternoon." Bucky responded.

***

"Hi Angel. You look terrific. Who is cutting your hair?"

"You look great yourself, Dr. Rosie. One of the deaf inmates, in prison for shooting her abusive husband and not being able to prove self-defense, is cutting, styling, and dying my hair. She is amazing. And I have you to thank because without learning American Sign Language, we would never have developed a relationship. Thank you again."

"That's fantastic. How many classes are left? Is there an advanced course?"

"We are four months into the six-month course. Taking it with Chappy has motivated me to work really hard. We practice a couple times a week. The deaf girls appreciate that we are trying to learn their language, really. They are patient with us now. We work together."

"How about your cooking classes?"

"Get this, Dr. Rosie. Chappy brought in a two-burner table-top, portable stove and of course she has a microwave and a small refrigerator in her office. We have made the soups that we have learned. They are tasty. Salads are easy but the ingredients are hard to get sometimes."

"And your groups? How have they been?"

"Amazing. The women are looking ahead and not caught up in their pasts and the awful labels that went with their lifestyles. The trafficked women will be protected when they are released. Maria will be returned to her family in Acapulco. Lydia and her brother will temporarily live with a Pastor and his wife in Manilla. And now that Maddie knows how to sew, she has a job as a seamstress at a department store, and lodging in a Christian rehab center where she can teach the teen-age girls to sew."

"What are your plans, Dr. Rosie?"

Rosie couldn't help but be amazed that Angel cares so much about her that she always wants to hear about her life and Bucky's. It feels so much like a two-way relationship.

"We are leaving next week for the Vienna Woods, Angel, where we will be supervising volunteers at Haus Edelweiss. That is where European pastors, secretly working on degrees from the United States come to complete courses."

"Oh, how I wish I could go with you. I will be thinking of you and praying for you, Dr. Rosie."

"I will come back to see you before Christmas again. Tomorrow, I thought I would bring you some thank you cards to send to the service sorority and anyone else you would like to show appreciation to. Would you like me to do that?"

"That would be really neat. I would love to do that. Do you think any of the ladies might want to write to me?"

"I am sure they will once you make personal contact. There are fourteen in their chapter. That's what you call their local group. I am sorry that I haven't heard back from anyone regarding a parole hearing. I will continue trying on your behalf and I believe the attorneys will do so as well."

"It's really okay, Dr. Rosie. Thank you for caring so much. I am blessed to have you as my friend. I know that God has a good plan for my life."

CHAPTER FIFTY

Angel's Stephen's Ministry

Dear Dr. Rosie,

Thank you for visiting me last week. I appreciate you taking your time during the holidays to come all the here. I have great news to share. I am no longer a supervisor in the sewing workshop. I completed my certification to be a Stephen's Minister. I think I mentioned that I was in training and that Chaplain Caroline has provided all the materials and supervision.

This means I will be assigned to women in the "hole". I told you that solitary confinement is called "the hole" by inmates. I will be working one on one with women there who are on suicide watch. I remember spending lots of time in solitary and it wasn't fun. I finally figured out how to control my emotions and not get assigned there anymore.

I can see how these women who hold their feelings inside can be depressed. I really want to encourage them and let them know I've been there too. I believe that will make them trust me, don't you?

I know it is because of you that I was able to take the American Sign Language classes on-line. I am pretty good at signing. It would be awful to be in solitary and be deaf. That would be the greatest send of isolation. There would be nothing to see but four gray walls and no sunlight.

Just wanted you to know, I pray for you and Bucky every day. If I could, I would make you the best chicken, lemon, rice soup in the world. Chappy and I invited Mrs. Marigold and Dr. Jo to have supper one cold night. They tasted the soup and loved it.

Thank you for arranging for the American Sign Language classes and the cooking classes. I sent thank you notes to the service sorority you connected me with. And I gave one to Chappy for helping to make it all happen.

Stay safe. And as I always say, sleep with the angels. You definitely are mine.

Love,

Angel

THE END

ABOUT THE AUTHOR

Phyllis Kuehnl-Walters, Ph.D.

Dr. Kuehnl-Walters, known as Phyllis Walters of The Villages Florida, is a retired clinical psychologist from Ohio. Third- and fourth-year medical students from the Ohio University School of Osteopathic Medicine completed their psychology rotations by observing and assisting in Dr. Walters' offices.

In addition to owning a large group practice in the Dayton area, she was an Adjunct Professor in several departments at the University of Dayton. She has also taught at the Life Long Learning College of The Villages, Florida. She has been a speaker in The Villages area churches and clubs as well as teaching and participating in women's Bible studies at Fairway Christian Church.

Dr. Walters became "refired" as an author in 2017 when she began writing Christian Inspirational books meant to encourage the reader to joyfully finish the race set forth by God. In 2019, she began another genre writing about cases she can never forget. Her first novel, "The Christmas Slayings," was inspired by an evaluation of a young woman charged with murder. Her second novel in the true crime/suspense genres is based on the cases of two women for whom she had compassion. Her third and fourth novels, "Husbands Who Kill" and "Kids Who Kill," are stories of men who committed crimes against women.

Dr. Walters is a member of the Florida Writers Association and The Writers League of The Villages. She is an Emeritus member of the Ohio Psychological Association and the American Psychological Association. She also belongs to The Women Doctor's Club of The Villages, Xi Rho Chapter of Sigma Phi Gamma International Service Sorority, and Fairway Christian Church of The Villages.

Dr. Walters states that she is blessed to have a balanced life as a mother, wife, Yaya, aunt, friend, beloved daughter, and sister. Writing is now her passion with the intent of inspiring others to understand their purpose in life, to believe, at any age, they are equipped to achieve it.

For speaking engagements, Dr. Walters can be reached at phylliswaltersauthor@gmail.com

REVIEWS OF EARLIER BOOKS

by
Phyllis K. Walters

The Christmas Slayings… A review by a follower who is eagerly awaiting the publication of Angel's Journey…"I only wish I could've been her attorney! I never loved a job so much and life in the courtroom with a judge and/or jury was heaven to me! You had to know the Judge, the Law, and you got to pick your own jury so on one could! It was the most rewarding job I ever had. Please send me a copy along with the bill and I will send you a check!" *D.G. Kettering, Ohio*

"The reader is allowed into her casework and her romance with the handsome Bucky Walker. The romance on the side helps soften the reality of these cases." *From Amazon – by J. J. Clarke, award-winning author of "Dared to Run," a suspense thriller.*

Wives Who Kill… "This well-written novel brings to light the very real and complex world of personal relationships where abusive partners or parents inflict damage upon those who they should be protecting. I look forward to reading Dr. Walter's next book." *From Amazon – by Mel Harrison, author of three suspense novels inspired by his experience in the foreign service of the United States of America.*

Husbands Who Kill … "Phyllis K. Walters skillfully helps the reader understand what makes…perpetrators do what they do with a mix of compassion, while she blends in some underlying humor to break up the seriousness of the subject." *From Sally Galliers, beta reader.*

Kids Who Kill…"Tragic story about a deaf young man with good intentions, evidenced by his attempts to help boys who he saw being victimized by bullies. What drove him to a life of crime? How would his life have been different if his father had recognized the abuse, he endured at boarding schools for the deaf? Dr. Walters needs to write a sequel about his time in prison with the other two young men from his past." *B.G., The Villages, Florida*

BOOKS

Also by Phyllis K. Walters, Ph.D.

The Christmas Slayings
Wives Who Kill
Husbands Who Kill
Kids Who Kill

Christian Inspirational Books
by
Phyllis Kuehnl-Walters, Ph.D.

Worry, Fret, and Fear…No More! (Covid-19 Edition)
A Six-week Challenge to Eliminate Worry and Overcome Fear.
Creating Balance: Purpose in Life…
Finding Joy and Meaning in this Season of Life.
Become a Beacon of Light…
Develop the Fruit of the Spirit and Reflect God's Love

DISCUSSION QUESTIONS

1. How many times did the legal system fail Angel Morgan? Who? Where? When?

2. How has Dr. Rosie's interest in Angel changed or influenced Angel's feelings about her circumstances and her future?

3. Three important characters are involved in Angel's life in prison: Daisy Marigold, Case Manager; Caroline "Chappy" Wexler; and Dr. Jo Andre, Medic. Which of the three do you most relate to and why?

4. What did you think of Officer Verna Mitchell and Chappy's relationships with Angel?

5. If Bonnie and Clyde Tipton had stayed under the radar, what might
They have done next as revenge toward Dr. Rosie Klein?

6. What did you think of the ways that Agents Cunningham and Thompson, along with Sheriff Holland, investigated and pursued the Tipton's?

7. Can you see how Angel Morgan, of all the defendants that Dr. Rosie evaluated, touched Rosie's heart from the beginning of their contact?

8. What do you see as the future for Bucky Walker and Rosie? Retirement?

9. In your opinion, should the Governor of Ohio commute Angel's sentence? If so, why? If not, why not?

10. If you were to write Angel a letter, what would you want to say to her?

NOTES

www.ingramcontent.com/pod-product-compliance
Lightning Source LLC
Chambersburg PA
CBHW060328260626
47160CB00007B/2722